A BRYSON FAMILY CHRISTMAS

BROTHERS IN BLUE, BOOK 4

JEANNE ST. JAMES

Jeanne ST. JAMES

Editor: Proofreading by the Page

Cover Artist: Golden Czermak at FuriousFotog

A huge thanks to my beta readers: Whitley Cox, Alex Schwab, Sharon Abrams, Andi Babcock

www.jeannestjames.com

Sign up for my newsletter for insider information, author news, and new releases: www.jeannestjames.com/newslettersignup

Warning: This book contains adult scenes and language which may be considered offensive to some readers. This book is for sale to adults ONLY, as defined by the laws of the country in which you made your purchase. Please store your files wisely, where they cannot be accessed by under-aged readers.

Keep an eye on her website at http://www.jeannestjames.com/ or sign up for her newsletter to learn about her upcoming releases: http://www.jeannestjames.com/newslettersignup

Author Links: Jeanne's Blog * Instagram * Facebook * Goodreads Author Page * Newsletter Jeanne's Review & Book Crew * Twitter * BookBub

Blood Fury MC, Dirty Angels MC and Blue Avengers MC are registered trademarks owned by Double-J Romance, Inc.

Dear readers,

Welcome back to Manning Grove, Pennsylvania. This book is solely an excuse to revisit with one of my favorite families, the Brysons. It was time to catch up and take a peek into their lives. If you're unaware, they also do cameos in my Blood Fury MC series, since that series is based in Manning Grove as well.

I hope you enjoy spending time once again with the Brysons as much as I enjoyed catching up with them myself. (I've missed them!)

Please be warned, Teddy and Adam are also included in this book so there are some sexy times happening between the engaged couple. If that's not your thing, you can always skip the end of chapter four when they have an intimate moment together (but I hope you don't).

If, for some reason, you missed Teddy and Adam's short story (which came after Matt's), you can download it here for free: BookHip.com/DRTBTW I highly recommend reading that before reading this book.

~ Jeanne (wishes she was a Bryson) St. James

PART ONE

CHRISTMAS EVE MORNING

CHAPTER ONE

MAX & AMANDA

The low, gravelly whisper filled her ear and made her nipples pebble. "You know what happens to bad girls who don't stay out of trouble?"

Amanda smiled and stretched, keeping her eyes closed. Her man's voice was delicious. "*Mmm.* Her husband spanks her ass."

"EWW, Mom! Gross!"

Amanda's eyes popped open and her ten-year-old daughter, Hannah, stood by the bed, her face twisted in disgust. She swallowed her thumping heart back into her chest.

"Why would Dad spank you?"

Oh shit. "He wouldn't," she lied as she sat up and noticed the other side of the bed was empty. "Where's your father?" Certainly not whispering naughty promises into her ear, *damn it.*

"Getting Liver and Greg ready."

Amanda pinned her eyebrows together. "Stop calling your brother Liver."

Her daughter huffed like only Hannah could. She was an expert at it. "That's his name."

"It is not. We picked out a perfectly good name."

"Then you should've had a perfectly good son. He's not. He needs to go back."

Her five-year-old son was never going back up her vagina. No way. No givebacks.

After Oliver was born, she'd pretty much threatened Max with death if he even *thought* about having a third child. She even had him get snipped. And if he didn't, she threatened to do it herself sometime during the night with a rusty butter knife.

Knowing his wife too well, he decided not to take that chance and made an appointment the next day.

Smart decision.

Two pregnancies were more than enough. The only good thing that came out of those were her two kids. Though, she was rethinking that right now as she frowned at Hannah, who stood with one hand on her hip.

She was ten going on sixteen. She took after her father.

Funny, he insisted Hannah was just like Amanda.

Well, at least they agreed she looked like Max with his dark brown hair and crystal blue eyes.

Amanda yawned. "What is he helping them with? Breakfast?"

"No, Mom! For Grandpa to pick us up."

"What?"

"It's an early Christmas present or something. That's what Dad was telling Liver."

"Hannah..."

Her daughter bugged her eyes out. She was an expert at that, too. She probably practiced the hand-on-hip, bugged-out-eyes routine in the mirror. "*Oooooliver*. There, you happy?"

Not really. "Whose Christmas present?"

Hannah shrugged. "Don't know."

"*I* don't know," she corrected her daughter.

"Apparently you don't, if you're asking me."

"Hannah." Amanda took a deep breath. Kids took a lot of patience. No one warned her of that before one of Max's enthusiastic swimmers hooked up with one of her reluctant eggs. "Say *I don't know.*"

"Okay. *You* don't know."

Amanda rolled her eyes. Her daughter did, too.

Oh lord, she was putting an ad in the local penny shopper and giving Hannah away. Cheap. *Screw it,* free.

Shit, she'd only find her way back home. The kid was pretty damn smart for ten. Plus, Max might not be happy that she gave away "Daddy's girl" and he might arrest his own wife.

Hmm.

That reminded her, they hadn't broken out the cuffs lately…

"Mom!"

"What?"

"Can I borrow your makeup?"

That was why her daughter interrupted her hot dream? "No. You're ten. And the last time you borrowed it—without permission, might I add—you ended up looking like a drunk raccoon."

Hannah snorted. "Well, if you'd teach me…"

"You're ten," Amanda reminded her for the millionth time. "Your father doesn't want you wearing makeup and we'll let him decide when you're allowed. Plus, if you haven't noticed, I'm not great at it."

"Teddy can teach me, then."

"Fine, go to Teddy. But not before your dad says it's okay."

"I'll ask him."

"Okay. Go do that now and stop asking me questions that you know I'm going to say no to before you even ask them."

"Whatever, Mom." She did her signature huff.

"Yeah, *whatever,*" she mimicked. "Now come here, give your mean mom a kiss and then go get ready to go to your grandparents. By the way, if Grandpa saw you with makeup on, he just might throw all your presents into the fireplace and then ground you for a month."

"He can't ground me."

"No? He still grounds your father and uncles."

Hannah giggled. "He does?"

"Yep. And since he outranks us all, he can ground anyone in the family."

"Even Grandma?"

"I'm sure Grandma gets a different type of punishment." She rolled her lips under, trying not to smirk.

"What kind?"

Oh shit. "Uh… that's between them."

"I'm going to ask him."

Oh shit! "No, you won't! That's… That's their business, not yours. Now, come give me a kiss since I won't see you until later."

"What's later?"

"The Christmas parade. Daddy's going to be up front right behind the mayor."

"He is?"

"Hannah, honestly, don't you pay attention to any of our conversations at dinner?"

"Yessss."

Amanda sighed. "Now you're fibbing."

"No worse than you," Hannah blurted out as she surged forward, gave Amanda a quick kiss on the cheek and bolted from the room.

Amanda stared at the empty doorway and smiled.

God, she loved that kid. She *might* have been worth all those hours of pain and torture—and the verbal abuse she gave Max—during her labor.

She should get up, take a shower and get ready for the day, but it was rare that the house was empty of not only the spawn from her loins, but her brother, Greg, too. She glanced at the clock. Another hour of uninterrupted sleep would be heaven.

She shimmied her way back under the covers and sighed as

she stretched out, having the whole king-sized bed to herself. Then closed her eyes and went searching for that dream...

"**Y**ou know what happens to bad girls who don't stay out of trouble?"

Max's wife stirred and a naughty smile crept over her face. "*Mmm.* Her husband— Wait, I'm not falling for that again." Her eyes popped open and she shot up in bed, smacking her head against his chin.

"Fuck!" they both shouted at the same time.

"Ow," Amanda moaned, rubbing the top of her head.

"Hey, your head is harder than my chin," he complained, rubbing his throbbing chin.

His wife not only had a hard head, she *was* a hardhead.

Her eyes raked down his naked body as he kneeled on the mattress next to her. The surprise in them quickly turned to heat.

That was more like it.

"Well, hello, Chief Bryson, I think you forgot your uniform. Do you at least have your cuffs since I'm a bad girl?"

Max raised an eyebrow. "I'm sure I can find a set somewhere in our bedroom. Is the cuff key still taped to the back of the headboard?"

"Why? Do you plan on wearing them?"

"Do you?"

"*Ooo.* That was an actual purr."

He wiggled his eyebrows. "You like that?"

She lifted a finger and tilted her head for a long moment. "You know what I like? Silence. No screaming. No fighting. No pounding feet up and down the stairs. No barking dog as Chaos tries to herd them. Greg not yelling out random *fucks* and *shits*. No glass breaking. No slamming of doors." She inhaled deeply through her nostrils, her eyelids fluttered shut and she exhaled a long, "*Aaaaaaah.*"

"Your extremely handsome husband's a genius to make it happen. Just admit it." He had suggested it to his parents, who jumped on the idea and decided to take *all* the grandkids—except for baby Levi—this morning and keep them overnight.

"An empty house might be the... Best. Christmas. Present. Ever!" She closed her eyes and flopped back onto the bed, her head bouncing off the pillows. "So freaking awesome."

"I know. Now you owe me."

"Mmm." She opened one eye. "But empty house or not, I'm not giving you another baby."

"It's been five years."

The other eye opened and she glared at him. "My dear, currently breathing husband who's at risk right now to be smothered to death, we are not having a baby every five years. After last time, I realized five years isn't long enough for me to forget. Everyone lied about that." She lifted a hand. "And, you forget how old I am now. *Way* too old."

"That's true."

Amanda jerked the pillow from under her head and whacked him with it. "You're not supposed to agree. And, anyway, you got snipped."

"If you remember, the doctor said it can be reversed. You know, in case I traded you in for a younger model." Max grinned and shrugged.

"I guess I'm putting an ad for both you *and* Hannah in the penny shopper."

"What?"

"Nothing," she muttered.

He sighed and reclined onto his side, facing Amanda and propping his head in his hand. "Listen, Levi coming into the family has made my paternal instincts kick in again."

"Paternal instincts to do what? Change shitty diapers? Clean up projectile vomiting? What? What part do you miss?"

"Well, the puking part we still deal with." Max swallowed down the saliva forming in his mouth. Sometimes he gagged just remembering about the god-awful messes their kids had made.

Amanda was also turning slightly green. "Okay, we need to stop talking about puke."

"Agreed. That's not what this was supposed to be about."

"What was?"

"Shipping them all off and getting some alone time with my wife."

"Mmm. That sounds better than babies. How long are they gone, again?"

"We won't see them again until they're opening presents under the tree at my parents'."

"What?"

Max's grin widened. "Yes... That's their Christmas present to us. A whole day and a whole night *alone*."

"Oh. My. God. Just the word *alone* makes me want to orgasm." Her hand slipped beneath the sheet.

"I already did," he said, wiggling his brows.

"*Ohhh*." Her brow furrowed. "Wait. The parade later..."

"Yeah, well, I'll be in it and you can hide from them. I'm sure we can find you some costume to wear so they don't recognize you."

Amanda laughed. "You know I'm using that for future blackmail."

"I'll deny it." He slipped his hand under the covers and ran it down her arm until he found where hers was. It was exactly where he thought. "But you can't deny me," he whispered.

"Well, I can. But before I trade you in on a new model myself, I'd like a ride in the old one."

"You may have to grease the rusty parts first."

Her lips twitched. "Same here."

For fuck's sake, he loved his wife. When he first encountered her by giving her a citation in the municipal parking lot, he never, ever thought over a decade later, they'd have two kids and a dog. She had been a spoiled rich brat—even she'd admit it—whose life had been turned upside down when she got guardianship of her special needs adult brother.

Worse, she had frustrated the hell out of him. But as she matured right before his eyes, he fell deeply in love with her and realized he couldn't live without her. Even though she pushed every one of his damn buttons. On purpose.

But now, she was a great mother, a successful small business owner and the perfect partner for him. Nobody could put up with his hardheadedness of being a cop and a retired Marine quite like her. Thank fuck she could.

He had been teasing when he said he wanted a third kid, but when he thought about it, Amanda being pregnant with his babies had been the most beautiful thing in the world.

Now those babies were no longer babies and were quickly developing into clones of their stubborn parents. At least they got it honestly.

Even so, life was good, and he was a lucky son of a bitch.

He was also about to get lucky with the woman who was pushing his hand between her legs. *As if* he needed encouragement. His finger slipped between her folds, finding her already wet.

He smiled.

"Do you want me to shower first?"

"Do you need to?" He hadn't yet. He'd been too busy getting the kids and Greg packed up and ready to head to his parents'.

"Well, you know... It's been a while since you've used your mouth and I just want to make sure you didn't forget your technique."

"It hasn't been that long," he scoffed.

She lifted a perfectly plucked brow. It should be perfectly plucked. She practically lived in one of the chairs at Manes on Main. Teddy probably put a bronze name plaque on one just for her.

"When was the last time?" she quizzed him.

He pursed his lips.

"Exactly," she said on a Hannah huff.

"*Welllllll*… We could do it in the shower, come back to the bed to do it again, and then do it in the shower a third time before the parade."

"And after the parade?"

"After the parade we are doing it on every surface on and in this fucking house."

She laughed and patted his cheek. "Look at you. Such confidence you can do it that many times in twenty-four hours. Such lofty aspirations."

"You'll be asleep after number two."

"I will not," she insisted.

"Then you'll have to forego any wine so you can make it to number three before you start snoring."

"Oh no. Sex pairs perfectly with a nice red."

He smiled. "Yes. A nice red, freshly spanked ass." He licked the tip of an invisible pencil. "I'll be putting that on the agenda."

"Oh my God. Are we now those fuddy-duddy type people who have to make an agenda for sex? Did we turn into them? Whatever happened to spontaneity?"

"Well. Greg happened. Then Hannah. And finally, Oliver," he reminded her.

"Mmm."

He leaned close and whispered, "But none of them are here. So, why are we wasting time?"

"Good point." She turned her head and gave him a quick kiss. "So, shower?"

"Remember the first time we were in that shower together?"

She pressed a fingertip to her lips. "You mean the night you purposely didn't tell me I was eating Bambi's dad?"

"That's the one," he answered. "We could recreate that. Minus the dinner."

"As long as we don't recreate the next morning. I was pretty pissed at you."

"Uh. You were a lot more than 'pretty pissed.' I had to grovel on my belly through hot coals and broken glass to get you back." That was a miserable time in his life. He'd been a stubborn idiot and almost lost her.

"You deserved it."

"I won't argue that. I was avoiding commitment and look at us now."

She laughed. "Yes, look at us now. Two old fuddy-duddies who have to have a long conversation before we have sex."

"Fine. We're not going to talk about it first, we're just going to do it. Let's make a pact that we're just going to spontaneously fuck whenever and wherever we want until tomorrow morning."

"Except for on the parade route this afternoon. We might get arrested by your own officers for indecent exposure, lewd acts, and corruption of minors."

"Okay, let's agree. We'll keep the indecent exposure and lewd acts under our roof."

"We haven't done it in your new truck yet, either," she reminded him.

He licked his invisible pencil again. "Okay, I'll amend that to include the driveway."

"And here we are talking about it again instead of doing it. We've already broken our pact."

"We start now. Deal?"

Amanda nodded. "Deal."

He grinned and took her mouth. He was done talking. Now was the time for action.

He sank the finger he'd been using to lightly strum her clit deep inside her. Her back arched and she sighed into his mouth.

Fuck, the sex with her had always been blazing hot. Even after all these years, it still was.

After seeing her in her tight, low cut jeans, high-heeled boots, and baby doll tee, striding across that parking lot with an attitude, he never looked at another woman again.

Not even in his dreams.

His wife was his fantasy come true. He could only hope he was hers.

He could only hope he could make her happy until her last breath.

He broke the kiss. "Baby..."

She pressed a finger to his mouth. "You know what I want you to do with that. And it's not talking."

He slipped his finger from her and rolled off the bed, heading toward the master bathroom.

"You're not going to caveman carry me?" she called out. He could hear the pout in her voice.

He paused and glanced back over his shoulder. "If I pull something in my back, that'll fuck up our plans. You want to risk it?"

Even though she muttered it under her breath, he still heard it. "See? I need that new and improved model."

"Yeah, but you love me," he insisted.

"I do love your ass. It's still perfect."

"Come and get it." He smacked his bare ass cheek and went into the bathroom to start the shower.

***

"I don't remember the shower being this small," his naked wife said as she climbed in, accidentally elbowing him in the gut.

"You shower in it every day. Okay, maybe not every day. Some days you take shower strikes." Max wrinkled up his nose.

"Very funny. I just mean with the two of us in it. Maybe we were more flexible back then."

"It wasn't that long ago, Mandy." He shuffled backward so she could get under the spray.

She sighed as the hot water hit her. "There's BC and AC. That first time was back in BC."

"Huh?"

She turned and backed her ass right into his cock. He was pretty sure it was by accident, but his cock didn't care.

"Before children and after children," she explained. "Your life is never the same in the AC years."

"If you want, we can put them up for adoption," he suggested.

She glanced over her shoulder, her auburn hair turning a dark brown as it got wet. "*Oooh.* Do you think anyone would notice?"

"The kids might." He shrugged. "I'm sure they'd get over it after a while. But then we'd lose our tax deduction."

"Damn," she whispered. "Now we *have* to keep them."

"Yeah, I think we're stuck with them."

She grabbed the body wash and just let it drop, landing right on the tip of his big toe.

"Hey! What did you do that for?"

She shrugged. "Well, I thought we were recreating that first time in this shower. Remember I dropped the soap? But at the time it was a bar of Dial, not a container of liquid gold you like from Bath and Bodyworks. You're much more sophisticated now."

"If you remember, the soap didn't land on my foot since I was standing outside the shower when you did that. Even so, we could have pretended instead of you maiming me. I also had clothes on and, being impatient for all of my sexy, irresistible manliness, you dragged me into the shower to ravish me."

"I did not."

"You did, too! You couldn't wait to get a piece of all this." He waved his hand over his wet body. For forty-four, he was in pretty damn good shape, if he said so himself.

And he still got plenty of compliments when he was in uniform. Yeah, maybe they all came from his mother, but who cared? Those counted, right?

"Actually, if I remember correctly, I was out running and you were stalking me, then you kidnapped me and brought me to your lair to ravish *me*."

"Can we just stick to our no-talking pact and get to the ravishing part?" he asked impatiently.

She ran a hand through her long, wet hair that stuck to her shoulders and back. Two kids and almost twelve years later, she was still as hot as when he'd brought her to his home for the first time.

Marriage and motherhood hadn't dimmed his desire for her. Their issue with having intimate moments was simply finding the time and privacy.

But they were guaranteed the next twenty-four hours and the clock was ticking.

Better yet, his cock was on board with the agenda.

He pushed her wet strands off one shoulder and drew his mouth over her damp skin, licking away some of the beading water until he got to her neck.

"Just so you know, you've ruined me for all other women," he murmured against her warm skin.

"That was my evil plan."

"You damn well succeeded." He nibbled up her neck, causing her to shiver, even under the hot spray.

She reached back and dug her fingers into his hair, letting out a little moan. That little noise made his cock flex against her ass.

Oh yeah, they had twenty-four hours, he might take her there, too. He'd have to remember to check to make sure they had lube. If not, there had to be something in the kitchen that would work.

"Hello?"

He *mmm*'d against her neck.

"You stopped nibbling. In your advanced age, did you lose track of what you were doing?"

"I didn't. I got distracted by thinking of all the wicked ways I can fuck my wife."

"*Oooh*. Last time I checked, *I* was your wife. I can't wait to experience all that wickedness. Will you remember your ideas?"

"Pretty sure I will. Have a feeling, afterward, you will, too."

She turned around almost knocking him backward, but he caught his balance. Barely.

Her hazel eyes were narrowed on him. "I don't like that grin."

He dropped his head until his lips were a hairsbreadth away from hers. "You forgot to pick up the soap."

"Mmm hmm. I know that trick."

His grin grew wider and he closed the gap between them, taking her mouth and exploring the recesses with his tongue. She wrapped her fingers around the back of his head and deepened the kiss with a moan that rose from within her.

Her beaded nipples brushed against his chest, teasing him. He cupped her breasts which were now bigger than when he first met her, and thumbed both nipples, drawing another moan from her.

He caught both between his fingers and slowly twisted them until she gasped into his mouth. He continued to twist until he knew it was to the point of painful and she finally broke the kiss, panting.

"Max," she whispered, her eyes hooded and full of heat.

Fuck yes, she was his.

At first, he had stubbornly denied it for months, until the thought of losing her drove him crazy. Then he realized he couldn't live without her.

And, fuck him, he couldn't.

They were done talking.

He backed her up against the shower wall and went down on his knees.

It wasn't to pick up the body wash.

Holy hell, he didn't remember his knees hurting the last time they did this. He pushed past the discomfort. "Hold on, baby."

Amanda grabbed his shoulders and he lifted her leg up over the arm he had braced against the tile, opening her thighs. With the other hand, he spread her pussy open.

Fuck yes, that glistening pink center was making his mouth water.

He licked and sucked the outer edges, his tongue sliding between them, tasting her. He tipped his eyes upward to see her head back against the wall, her eyes closed and a smile on her face as the water beaded on her skin.

He wanted that smile gone, her shouting his name and the result of her orgasm on his lips. He sucked harder on her clit until she jerked against him and a low, long, "*Ohhhh*," came from between lips that were no longer curled upward but parted, instead.

That was more like it.

With a tilt of her hips, she gave him better access to stroke her slick slit with one finger while scraping his teeth lightly over her hard, sensitive nub.

"Max," she breathed.

Fuck yes.

His cock was hard and throbbing and his balls tight with knowing she was getting wetter and soon he would get the chance to lose himself within her slick heat.

He slipped two fingers inside her and curved them, finding the spot that drove her wild, her hips following each deliberate stroke.

He knew how to get his wife tuned up. Knew what she liked, what she loved, what she wanted and needed. He was only happy to give it to her, because she gave him all of the same.

He kept strumming as he flicked her clit with the tip of his tongue and felt her clench around him. Her breathing had become ragged, her nails now dug sharply into the flesh at his shoulders, but he didn't let up.

"Yes," she hissed. "Max... Keep... Keep... Don't stop."

He had no plans on stopping, not until she came, not until she was good and primed for his cock so he could take her directly to orgasm number two.

He didn't think he could wait to get to the bed to slide inside her. No, he would take her in the shower before the water got too cold and then take her again in the bed.

For the next twenty-four hours, they'd make the most out of the gift they were given. Max might have to send his parents on a cruise as a thank you. He was pretty sure his brother, Marc, would pitch in since they were kid-free, too. Sort of. They couldn't pass off one of them to the grandparents. But then, the child not being born yet was a good reason for it.

However, that wasn't his concern. His focus was solely to get Amanda to hurry up and come so he could get them both there for her second time.

He reached up and tweaked a nipple as he sucked her clit more roughly, occasionally scraping it with his teeth as he drove his fingers home over and over.

Then she was there. Her back arched, her fingernails practically tore his skin and she cried out so loudly, the acoustics in the shower made it deafening.

But he didn't give a shit. She could make him bleed, give him hearing loss, smother him to death between her thighs, it was all worth it.

All of it.

And when she was done, when the last ripple ebbed away, she drooped against the wall, dropped her head and stared down at him as he smiled up at her.

She smiled back and asked the same question she asked all those years ago. And it was just as breathless. "Was it as good for you as it was for me?"

"Better than I remember."

"What did we do next?"

"We ate."

"You just did, but I could eat." Her voice was soft and suggestive, and it made his balls tighten even more. Precum was escaping from his cock as fast as it was being washed away by the water.

He could not wait a whole meal to be inside his wife.

He stood. Slowly. His knees cracking as he did so. As soon as he could smooth away the wince, he asked, "What are you hungry for?"

"You," she said simply with a lazy smile.

He ran his thumb over her wet bottom lip. "I want to fuck you."

"You will. But I need to satisfy my hunger first and then we can have breakfast before you take me to bed and remind me of why I married you in the first place."

He lifted an eyebrow and grabbed the root of his cock. "You only married me for this?"

"It was the main selling point." She pushed his hand away, grabbed it in her fist, giving it a good squeeze, and brushed her thumb across the crown.

As she went to her knees, he warned, "Once you get down there, it's hard getting back up. Just give a signal if you need help."

She tipped her face up to him. "Like the bat signal?"

"Just a simple 'help' would work."

She pinned her lips together for a second before she dropped her head and took him fully into her mouth.

"Holy shit," he breathed, digging his fingers into her soaked hair.

She'd take him deep, then, as she slid her mouth upward, she'd swirl her tongue around the head of his cock before swallowing him almost whole again.

"Baby," he groaned, his fingers twitching in her hair, resisting the urge to thrust.

He fought closing his eyes because he wanted to watch her. The way her head bobbed, the way her lips stretched around him, the way her fist squeezed the root, making the veins pop.

It was beautiful.

Mind-blowing.

Sexy as fuck.

He fisted her hair tighter and began to shift his hips just slightly, not wanting to full-out face fuck her.

Okay, he did want to, but knew from experience that could get ugly and could ruin the moment. So, he started with very shallow thrusts as her tongue swirled and licked and stroked along the thick ridge.

Jesus, if he let her keep going she was going to suck his brains right out of his cock.

He didn't need his brains anymore, did he?

Hell no.

He couldn't remember the last time she'd blown him like this. Most of the time, they were barely lucky enough to have undisturbed sex. So, to have her take her time and do this...

Christmas needed to come more often.

Once a month.

Twice a month.

Oh fuck. She gently worked his balls as she ran her lips up the underside of his throbbing cock. She squeezed the root tighter and slid her hand up the length, milking another thick, shiny drop of precum from it.

And *fuuuuuuuuckkkkk.* She lifted her eyes to his, stuck out her hot, pink tongue and licked it right off the tip like a melting ice cream cone.

He tried to swallow but his throat was tight as she once again slid him all the way into her wet, hot mouth, sucked hard and then pulled back until just the crown was between her lips.

She smiled.

"Fuck, baby," came out in a groan. He got a better grip on her hair and began to thrust as far as her fist at his root allowed him.

But it was enough.

Holy hell, it was more than enough.

"'Manda," he warned. Though, he was clenching his jaws so tightly he had to force it out.

He didn't know if she tried to answer him around his cock or she simply hummed, but either way, she vibrated around him as her fingers worked his balls, and...

And...

He slammed a hand onto the shower wall, dropped his head, shoved his hips forward one more time and came deep at the back of her throat. His cock pulsed and pulsed, expelling cum in hot jets. She did not release him, instead she accepted it all.

Even after he had stilled, she slowly worked him in and out of her mouth, until he was empty.

Completely fucking empty.

He sucked in oxygen and opened his eyes just in time to watch her let him slip from her mouth. He let the cooling water rinse him off as he offered her a hand. She took it and he pulled her to her feet and into his arms.

"Love you, Mandy."

She reached up and cupped his cheek. "Love you, too. Now turn off the water before we get hypothermia. Then my husband is going to make me a big pot of coffee and an even bigger breakfast for that expert head I just gave him."

"I'll make you an awesome dinner tonight, too, if I can have a repeat performance for dessert."

"Not being greedy at all, are we?"

"Oh, fuck yes. I'm being so, so greedy. We both should be."

"Mmm." She grabbed his face with both hands and pulled him down to her, kissing him hard. "Then let's dry off, you make breakfast while I dry my hair and then we can get cracking on that."

She released him and as she stepped out of the shower, he turned it off and followed her.

The sharp crack of his palm against her wet ass sounded like a gunshot in the bathroom. He couldn't resist doing it when she reached for her towel. Her ass was just so tempting.

"Hey!"

"Buck up, buttercup. This is just the beginning."

"Don't start what you can't finish," she warned him.

"Oh, being feisty, are we?"

"I had a dream you were going to spank me and our—one of those small people we won't mention right now—interrupted me."

"You haven't been in trouble lately."

"Oh, I need to be bad? I can arrange that. I was always good at being bad."

He grabbed his own towel, paused in front of her, pressed his lips to hers and murmured, "And always bad at being good, but if you want a good spanking, all you have to do is ask," against them.

"And you will do your duty as a good husband and discipline your wife."

"Damn, I like the sound of that." Max finished drying off and wrapped the towel around his waist as his wife moved to the vanity and grabbed a hairdryer. "Meet you at the breakfast table."

"Make sure you make lots of carbs, Max. You're going to need them," she called out as he left the bathroom. "Along with loads of caffeine so you don't fall asleep."

"Got it. Coffee and French toast coming right up." With a grin, he took one last glance at Amanda standing in front of the mirror totally naked, drying her hair. And then he forced himself to get dressed and make them breakfast.

"Just so you know, when I see you later all hot and handsome in your dress uniform riding on the back of that convertible, I'm going to remember this moment and have a mini-orgasm."

The metal cuffs rattled. "This only rates a mini?"

"Well, I don't want to be too obvious when I have it. I only want you to *think* about me having it as you're up there waving at the citizens that you protect and serve."

"That's evil."

Amanda grinned as she rose up on his cock and paused at the very top. "Then you can punish me later." She slid back down *slowly*, knowing it was torturing him to go at that pace.

Max blew out a loud breath.

Being a type-A, purely alpha male of both the cop and Marine variety, he rarely let her cuff him to the bed. And before he did, he'd checked three times to make sure a cuff key was taped behind the headboard where he could reach it.

But since she was currently riding his cock, he had no complaints about being restrained. In fact, he had welcomed it so he could do it to her later. She was fine with him doing it to her, too, since she trusted him one hundred percent. And the man had some mad skills in bed.

Another reason she wore his ring.

But right now, she was in control, even though his legs weren't bound in any manner and it wouldn't take him long to get free if he was determined to shift that control.

She wouldn't complain about that, either. She loved when her husband went all caveman on her. Gripping her hair and ripping her head back, biting and sucking hard enough to leave marks and then fucking her so hard, she could hardly catch her breath.

Hell yesssss...

Max groaned as that thought had made her clench tight while she ground herself against his lap, driving his cock deeper.

He bent his knees and planted his feet into the mattress, tilting her forward. Without a word between them, she knew what he wanted. Sliding her hands over his still hot-as-hell chest and up his well-defined, restrained arms pulled over his head, she leaned forward until one of her nipples was barely touching his lips. She slid the tip along the seam of his mouth, tempting him.

He resisted for only a second before a little growl escaped him and he captured it, sucking it hard. It was like his lips pulled a sensual string connected from her nipple all the way to her pussy, and she tightened around him again as she lifted and fell.

"Fuck, baby," he mumbled against her flesh.

"No talking. Keep doing... *Yesss*... that." Their eyes connected as he continued to wreak havoc on her sanity. Those crystal blue eyes had caught her attention so long ago, and still made her melt as she stared into them.

Gripping his wrists, she began to move faster and in response, his attention to her breasts turned rougher. Nipping, sucking, scraping, licking.

God, she loved when he gave her breasts his full attention. He had control of those while she kept control of his cock, using it to work herself to a crescendo.

"Max," she whimpered, unable to stop her eyes from closing to just lose herself in the pleasure he was giving and she was taking.

A sharp bite made her open her eyes. And, again, no words were needed. They knew each other that well. She locked hers with his again and continued to ride him hard and fast. His attention to her nipples became more intense and he tensed beneath her.

He was close.

Luckily, so was she.

"Max," she whimpered again, struggling to keep her eyes on his as the pressure built within her, within him. His cock got even harder as he most likely struggled to wait on her.

But he didn't have to wait long.

She cried out as her pussy pulsated around his twitching cock. They managed to come at the same time and she kept riding him, but slowed the pace until she was done, he was done and the only thing left was their heavy breathing and racing hearts.

As he released her peaked nipple, she collapsed on him with a satisfied smile, not caring his body was damp with sweat, because so was hers.

That just gave them another excuse to share the shower before they both headed off to the Christmas Parade.

CHAPTER TWO

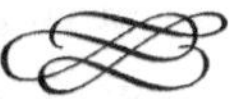

MARC & LEAH

"Are they gone?" Leah asked as she stepped out of the bathroom for what seemed like the hundredth time.

"Yes, I did a drop and dash. I opened the front door, shoved them in and slammed it shut behind them."

Leah laughed. "Father of the Year material right there."

"Did you want me to stay and jaw with my parents? Maybe sit down for breakfast with them, Greg, Hannah and Oliver? Breakfast smelled pretty damn good."

"No. You did good. Brownie points for you. But are you hinting that I can't cook as well as your mother?"

"Not hinting, Leah. Outright stating it."

She moved farther into the bedroom. "I don't have time to cook anymore since I'm a full-time cop and mother, Marc. Neither are easy jobs."

"You used to be a beast in the kitchen."

She walked over and stood belly to belly with her taller husband. At over six months along, she was showing pretty good now. "Wouldn't you rather me be a beast between the sheets?"

His lips twitched. "Can't you be both?"

She sighed and patted his chest. "You're awfully demanding."

The twitch turned into a wicked smile. "Why are you still wearing clothes? I figured I'd come home to find you naked in bed as my reward for getting rid of the boys."

She pointed both index fingers to her rounded belly. "Look, if you haven't noticed, I'm carrying your kid."

"I noticed."

"I don't move as quickly as I normally do. And, might I remind you, it wasn't my choice to get knocked up a third time."

Marc smothered a laugh.

Leah raised a brow. "I'm glad you find it funny. But you won't be laughing if it's not a girl this time." Leah was crossing her fingers and toes for a girl. Boys were stinky creatures.

"Hate to tell you, I only shoot boy sperm. Took after Pop."

He did *not* just puff out his chest at that! "There are enough boys in this family already. In fact, way too many."

"Can't have enough Bryson testosterone on this Earth."

"I think most of us would disagree."

"It made me irresistible to you."

She pressed a finger to her lips and tilted her head. "Hmm. Did it?"

"If I remember correctly, you would stare at me inappropriately while we were on coach-pupil training."

She rolled her eyes. "*Anyway*, this is it." She made a scissor motion with her fingers directly in front of his face. "Snip. Snip. Just like Max."

"Max didn't want to do it. He was threatened with bodily harm."

"And I know how to physically subdue a threat. Don't make me use that knowledge. I'll pin you down, borrow Amanda's rusty butter knife and do it myself."

Marc winced and grabbed his balls over his sweat pants.

Gray, she noticed. Her favorite pair, as long as he wasn't strutting down Main Street in them.

Men in uniform or gray sweatpants tended to catch a woman's

eye. And it didn't matter if he wore a wedding band or had two sons and another baby on the way.

Plus, her man was super handsome and sexy.

Damn it, he was right. He was irresistible. Even after all these years.

But there was no way in hell she was telling him that. He'd strut around the room and crow like a dick... *err*... a cock.

"Anyway, three is plenty. We don't have room in this house for more. Plus, if this is a boy—and it better *not* be—that means I'll have four male children to deal with. My sanity might be compromised between the smell, the burps and the farts. From both the two-legged and the four-legged children."

Two young boys, one man-child and two Mastiffs made their house a disaster on a daily basis.

She never should have let Marc talk her into stopping her birth control.

Never.

He had caught her at a weak moment.

"Not only that, every time I go on maternity leave the department is short-handed. That's not fair to the rest of you."

"Not this time with Max hiring Bridget."

"I don't think your cousin likes being called that."

"I know she doesn't, but it's weird calling a woman Jet."

She lifted an eyebrow. "You call her what she wants to be called. Or have you forgotten the hard lesson you learned about equality. Do you need a reminder?"

Marc lifted a hand. "Nope. I'm good."

"Well, with Jet coming to the department, I'm not rushing to go back this time. Whatever time Max gives me, I'm taking."

"I don't like you working at all while you're pregnant."

She patted her husband's chest. "Then, good thing it's not up to you."

"You're my wife and the mother of my kids."

"And that doesn't make me any less of a person. I can still make my own decisions. Since I'm six months along, your brother will soon have me sitting desk, anyway. I want to work until that happens. Sitting desk is *borrrrrring.*"

"It's safer."

"Manning Grove isn't a war zone, Marc."

"No, but things do happen—as we both know all too well—and I just don't want you or the baby to get hurt."

"We won't."

He put his thumb under her chin and lifted her face to his. "I don't want anything to happen to you or the baby."

She gave him a soft smile. "I know. And I love you for that. But I wanted to be a cop and knew what it entailed. Being a mother doesn't make me stop being that cop."

He couldn't hide his struggle from his face. He wanted to argue, but after all these years, he knew better. It was the same argument they had when she was pregnant with Austin and Jackson. He lost those, too.

Even though Max had been concerned with her doing patrol and taking incidents while she carried his nephews, he was smart and bit his tongue. He put being a chief before being Leah's brother-in-law, which was why he was so damn good at his job. He was a good leader for their department and an even better brother-in-law.

"So, the boys know not to come home, right?" she asked.

"I put the Invisible Fence collars around their necks, so they can't get past my parents' front yard without a good zap."

Leah knew he was kidding, but played along. "Oh, that's perfect. We have almost twenty-four hours to do what we want."

"No, you have almost twenty-four hours. I need to work second shift today. I'll be working the parade and then doing patrol afterward."

"That's right." She pouted because she didn't want to gloat at the fact she would get the house to herself for hours. *Hours!* That never happened. She might even roll around on the carpet naked, reveling in the fact she was *alone*, just like Menace and Trouble did when the dogs found deer shit out in the grass.

"How you managed to get off that detail is beyond me."

She shrugged one shoulder. "Max likes me better than you."

"Anyway... Since our time is limited, can we have sex now?"

"Can we fuck instead?" she asked.

He frowned. "What's the difference?"

She tilted her head and gave him a knowing look. "You know the difference."

"We always fuck. That's how you got knocked up three times, remember?"

She rolled her eyes. "No, whenever we get the opportunity, we have sex. Right now, the house is empty and I want to fuck like we used to." She sighed. "What happened to us, Marc? We used to be wild and crazy in bed."

"Kids happened," he said simply with a shrug.

"Yes, kids happened. They changed everything."

"Not everything." He tipped his head down and his light blue eyes were serious. "I still love you. Do you still love me?"

She frowned. "Of course. Isn't it obvious? I never want us to simply exist. I want you to *know* I love you, to feel it without saying the words. I hope you do because I never want you to question how I feel about you as my lover, my husband, the father of our children and their role model, too."

He smiled and cradled her face. "Truth? I never thought I wanted kids until you, Leah. Then there was nothing I wanted more. With you and only you."

"You told me that every time you got me pregnant."

"I got *you* pregnant? I remember being tied up plenty of times while you rode my cock until my balls were drained dry. I'm surprised I didn't become pregnant."

"Now that's a concept I could go along with. Men carrying the babies. Let them suffer the sore back and swollen feet, the hemorrhoids, the labor. Though, the human race would expire if that happened."

"Won't argue that. We would have zero children if I had to shit out a watermelon."

"Mmm. Watermelon. I could go for some right now." Her cravings were crazy with this pregnancy compared to the last two.

"Okay, let's stay on topic here... Which is us getting naked and pretending we're childless and having wild and crazy sex."

Her hand went to her distended belly. "Well, we might not be able to get too crazy, but we can do really naughty things to each other."

"Yes!" He did a fist pump. "I'm on board with that."

"Then why are we standing here?"

"Because you were supposed to be naked and waiting in our bed when I dumped off the boys."

"Oh."

"Yeah, oh."

She dropped her gaze to the outline of his erection. "And that is why I love those sweatpants."

"And why you forbid me to wear them off the farm."

"I didn't forbid you, I strongly advised against it."

"Uh huh. My wife packs a gun and a Taser, I take her strong advisement seriously."

She leaned toward him. "As you should." She pressed her lips to his and slid her hand over his hot and thick hard-on beneath the soft cotton. She dipped her tongue between his lips and tangled it with his. His cock flexed against her fingers and she was tempted to dig it out and go to her knees. Unfortunately, she wasn't sure she'd be able to get back up.

She pulled away just enough to say, "If I wasn't already pregnant, I'd take this so-called gift your parents gave us and think they were only doing it so we'd have another baby."

"Maybe. But right now they're content because they can smell all the new baby scent they want with Levi."

She reluctantly released him and stepped back. "They are going to have their hands full watching this one," she pointed to her belly, "and Levi at the same time. Your father might have to help with diapers if they're babysitting them together."

"My pop's a retired cop and a Marine, he's used to handling shit."

"Oh, you do know I'll use that line on you when it comes time to change the baby's diaper and she's had an explosion."

Marc faked a gag. "No. I put my foot down on those up the back explosions."

"Maybe you should take paternity leave and I'll go back to work right away."

"You need to nurse him."

"I don't *need* to nurse *her*. I can pump. Just like Autumn is doing for Levi. We'll buy you one of those breastfeeding harnesses and *you* can breastfeed her."

"Why are we still standing here talking and not fucking?"

"Now you're just trying to change the subject."

"Not trying, I am. Get naked, wife, while I dig out our dusty toy chest."

Her brow rose. "*Ooo.* Where do we start?"

"Wherever my loving wife wants to start."

Ass kisser. "A butt plug up your ass."

"Okay, not there."

"Electrodes to your balls."

"Not there, either."

She laughed. "Then you lied."

"I will amend my statement. Wherever my loving wife wants to start *and* I agree with her suggestion... since she's a closet sadist."

"That's no fun."

"Besides, we don't have a butt plug or electrodes."

"Are you sure? Do you want to test that theory?"

He grimaced. "No."

"Smart, because you tend to learn lessons the hard way."

He clapped his hands together. "Okay! Get naked, get on the bed, I'll grab the toy box and we'll get this party started."

"That sounds super romantic."

"Wait, we're being romantic? You said you wanted to fuck."

"True. Romance is overrated, anyway. Multiple orgasms are better than sweet whispers of your love and devotion to me."

His mouth dropped open. "Multiple?"

Of course that was the only part he picked up on. "I think I want to return your parents' gift. This is not turning out like I'd hoped. Did they give you a gift receipt?"

Marc snorted and went to the closet, opening it and digging through some shoeboxes stacked on the top shelf. Out of the reach of curious, sticky little fingers. Or four-legged monsters who would think a latex butt plug was a chew toy.

"Fuck yes!" she heard from inside the closet.

He backed up a step with a box in his hand. "I think this is it."

"Open the lid to make sure it's not a pair of your old, stinky sneakers."

"I prefer the surprise element. You stick your hand in it and pull something out. Whatever you choose, we're doing."

"*Ooo.* I like this game."

"Right? Wait." He lifted the lid and peeked inside. "You didn't sneak a butt plug in there, did you?"

"No cheating!" she yelled.

"Yes, this is the box. Though, I'm not sure where the stuff is that never fit in this box."

"Like the sex swing? I think that went up in the attic after Austin was born."

Marc glanced up at the ceiling. Her gaze also rose, spotting the eyebolts where they used to hook it. His eyes dropped back to her and a wicked grin crossed his face.

"No," she said immediately. "I'm too awkward right now. And if it crashed to the floor, it might hurt the baby."

The grin morphed to a grimace. "Okay. Next Christmas."

"Let's just get through this one first, please."

"You're not naked, yet."

"Neither are you!"

He dropped the box on the bed, yanked the Manning Grove PD sweatshirt over his head, threw it over his shoulder, then shucked his sweatpants and boxer briefs at the same time, dropping them to his bare feet.

He grabbed his cock and stroked it. "My wife is once again wrong. I am totally naked. It's she who is not."

Leah laughed and began to peel the camisole up over her belly. It fit like a second skin because Marc hated when she hid her body with anything loose, like normal maternity clothes. And she didn't mind wearing the camisoles because that meant she didn't have to wear a damn bra.

The less she wore when she was off-duty, the better. Being in uniform tended to be stifling some days. Especially when she was pregnant.

"A little help," she asked as one of her larger-than-normal breasts got hung up in the built-in shelf-bra.

"I don't know, baby, having you bound like that is giving me some ideas."

"I'm not bound, I'm being smothered by cotton and Lycra." The rest of the pink cami covered her head.

"I like it. I have full access to these puppies." Fingers tweaked her sensitive nipples.

"Marc."

"Yeah?"

"You have nipple piercings for a reason. I can't play with them if I'm stuck in this cami."

"Good point." He helped her get it the rest of the way off. "By the way, if I get a Prince Albert, will you play with that, too?"

As her head was freed, she cringed. "You are not sticking a big needle through the end of your cock. Because if something goes wrong, I'm out a cock and would need to find a new one. Just saying." Just the thought of a man piercing the head of his penis gave her the willies.

"Another very good point since you're stuck with mine."

"Hmm. That's debatable."

He grabbed her chin and lifted it. "No, it isn't. You're stuck with me for life, remember? 'Til death do us part?"

"Oh. I think I missed that part because of Teddy strutting around during our wedding trying to attract Adam with a peacock mating dance. It was very entertaining."

"You mean you didn't hear the part where you were to obey me?"

She knew those words had been removed from the vows. "Can't say I did."

"Well, you agreed right there in front of witnesses. So, you can't back out of that contract. You're stuck with me until death and you must obey me."

"We shall see."

"You still have pants on."

She hooked her fingers into her PJ bottoms and shoved them down, along with her panties. "Not anymore."

"That's more like it."

Leah stretched. "It's so nice to be naked and not worry about the boys barging in. I might stay that way until we need to go over to your parents' tomorrow morning."

"You have the parade."

"Do you think anyone would mind?" she asked.

"You might get frost bitten."

"Then I'll just stay home."

"No. Mom and Pop might need help with the kids and Greg."

"Greg is good with the kids."

"Greg *is* a kid," he reminded her.

Even at thirty-two years old, Amanda's special needs brother was just as much of a kid as the rest. He always had a blast playing with the boys. And their boys loved Greg to death. So did Hannah and Oliver. Greg was more like their sibling than uncle.

"Just go, please," Marc pleaded. "I'll be walking the crowd, but the three boys and Greg are a lot for them to handle and they won't admit it."

"I'm sure Amanda and Carly will be there. And Teddy."

Marc tipped his head. "Adam, Matt and I will be working so we can have Christmas Day off."

"Wait, when is *the thing?*"

"The thing?"

"What Adam has planned."

"Tomorrow."

"We all need to be there."

"We will. Everyone without the name of Bryson is taking shifts tomorrow just for that reason, you know that."

"Oh yeah. Baby brain." That's right, everyone else on the force was stepping in so none of them had to work Christmas. Though, the shifts would be light since Christmas was usually a slow day.

Hopefully that remained true tomorrow.

He pressed a hand to her belly. "After this one you can't use that excuse anymore."

"I won't need that excuse, remember?"

He opened his mouth and then snapped it shut. "Why aren't we having sex yet?"

"*Fucking.* We're fucking."

"We're not fucking, that's the problem. We're standing here naked having a damn conversation. The clock is ticking. Tick. Tock."

He reached over and grabbed the box, holding it out. Leah slipped her hand under the lid and grabbed the first thing her fingers touched. She pulled it out and held it up.

Marc's eyes lit up. Probably because it wasn't a butt plug.

"That's waterproof," he whispered, staring at the vibrating cock ring.

"And?"

"And... when's the last time we got naked in the Jacuzzi tub?"

"You mean together? Before Austin was born, I think."

"I think it's time to give it some use. But what I want to do first, we'll do here, since I don't want to drown."

Oh, she knew what that meant. Marc was going *down*.

She tried not to squeal with excitement. If she did, he would think she bonked her head. "We'd need to fill the tub in the meantime."

"I'll get it started. You get on the bed. I haven't eaten breakfast yet and I'm really fucking hungry. Get it ready for your husband."

"Normally, I'd be making you rethink that little demand, but since I'm agreeable with your plan, I'll allow it." She climbed onto the bed.

"Be right back." He rushed into the master bathroom.

Leah grabbed the shoebox and knocked off the top, digging around in it and finding the chain she used to use all the time to hook onto his nipple rings. She quickly tucked it under the pillows she had propped up for her to lean against.

She dug around some more and found some gel that warmed the skin and then when you blew on it, cooled it. It was specifically for oral play. She threw that on the comforter. She also pulled out the ostrich feather.

She left the cuffs and the other toys in the box, covered it and put it on the nightstand close by, just in case they were inspired to play again after he got home from his shift. Though, as tired as she'd been lately, she might not be awake when he came home.

Which was a good reason to take advantage of their time now.

The water began to run in the large Jacuzzi tub. The tub they hardly used because they didn't have time to lounge around and soak. Instead, they usually showered before or after work. It sounded like he didn't open the faucet all way, which meant they didn't have to rush and worry about the tub overflowing.

Leah leaned up against the pillows she'd stacked, and spread her legs wide with her knees bent. She grabbed the sensitizing lube, and after opening it, dabbed it onto her clit. Immediately, it began to stimulate her and heat up.

Oh yeah. They needed to keep it within arm's reach in the nightstand. She forgot how good that stuff was. Her pussy clenched tight as her clit got even hotter.

As he was coming back into the room, she rubbed some of the cherry-flavored gel on each nipple as he watched.

His blue eyes darkened and his cock, which was once again hard as a rock, flexed. He grabbed it and began to stroke. "Keep touching yourself." His voice was a little hoarse and his Adam's apple jumped as she did as he demanded.

The power during sex went back and forth between them. He knew what turned her on and she knew the same about him.

She knew his limits and he knew hers. In the beginning, they had spent a lot of time exploring those limits. It was nice to have a trustworthy partner to do that with.

And she trusted Marc.

Not from the moment they first met. Hell no. He'd been an unapologetic misogynist and believed that women didn't belong in law enforcement. She had to work hard and stay even stronger during her time with him as her Field Training Officer to prove otherwise. Not only show she could do her job as well as any other male in the profession, but she was an equal, that she could be his partner during and outside of work.

When he finally trusted her, she finally trusted him.

Completely.

They also found that their strong attraction to each other was much more than sex. Though, the sex was awesome, too. More than awesome. Their sexual desires were perfectly in sync. She'd never had that before. Neither had he.

She kept circling both nipples, the tips hard, the warmth from the gel spiraling through her, through her belly and down to her warm clit.

She released one nipple and touched her clit, making everything on her twitch.

"Marc," she whispered, turning her eyes to him. She might come without him. In the second trimester, she was always hornier than usual. That was why she kept a vibrator in the nightstand on her side of the bed. Okay, more than one. She had a variety for when Marc was working opposite shifts and she needed to take off the edge. But she usually had to wait until the boys were sleeping soundly.

However, this morning they could get loud and not worry about being interrupted or heard.

Yessss...

Marc moved to the end of the bed, still stroking his cock intently, his eyes glued to her finger circling her pulsating clit. Trickles of arousal tickled her folds.

She pointed to a nipple. "Taste these before that." Her demand sounded throaty and his hand moved even faster. "Don't you dare come. I have plans for that."

He grimaced, immediately released his cock, moved onto the bed and to her side. As she continued to play with one dark pink nipple, he sucked the other deep, scraping it with his molars, the heat of his mouth on the gel creating a pleasurable burn against her flesh. She groaned and pressed harder against her clit, using two fingers now.

He knocked her hand away from her other nipple and took that one into his mouth, heating it up, then he blew lightly on the tip and a shiver went through her as his breath created a cooling sensation. He went back and forth from one nipple to the other, and the one that was lacking attention from his mouth was between his two fingers as he twisted and pulled, drawing a guttural groan from her.

She wanted to throw her head back, close her eyes and just concentrate on the sensations surging through her. Instead, she kept them focused on her husband because he kept his ice blue eyes tipped to her.

So damn gorgeous.

Her toes curled and her muscles became tight as her orgasm built.

He was not gentle with her nipples. He licked, sucked and bit the flesh, not caring if it left marks, driving her to where he wanted to take her. Where she wanted to go.

Then she arrived.

He did not let up as her hips surged and her climax made her gasp and release her sensitive clit. Digging her fingers tightly into his hair, she pulled his head off her breast and pushed it down her body.

He didn't even hesitate. He settled between her bent legs and immediately put his mouth on her even before the last ripple disappeared.

She brushed her thumbs over the now overly-sensitive nubs of her nipples as he sucked and flicked his tongue between her legs and used his breath to both heat and cool her clit, which was still affected by the gel.

Once again, an intense wave rushed through her and she cried out his name. She cupped her breasts, kneading, and he sucked her gently once the second orgasm was done.

Her body went weak and loose as if she was a marionette whose strings were cut. She simply breathed as Marc pressed his forehead to the top of her mound, his breath also very ragged.

Until it wasn't.

He sucked in a sharp breath and jerked as if someone had shocked him. "Uh... I know that's not your tongue licking my balls right now."

They both glanced at the end of the bed to see Trouble, their one-year-old female Mastiff, with her two big front paws on the bed and looking quite pleased with herself.

"What the fuck!" Marc shouted and scrambled away from her and off the bed. "Gross."

Leah smothered her snort as she dropped her head back to the pillow. "*Sooo*, is now an appropriate time to remind you that besides baby number three, it was you who also wanted beast number two? That's what you get."

"Trouble, get out!" He pointed to the door. The Mastiff took her time lumbering in that direction, so he grabbed her collar and pulled her along faster. As soon as he pushed her out of the room, he slammed the door shut and turned. "Menace is old. Having Trouble will ease the pain when he... *goes*."

"For you or the boys?"

"For all of us. I know they sleep in bed with you when I'm doing a late shift. I find dog hairs in the sheets. Not to mention slobber on my pillows."

"You've got an active imagination, you know that? That doesn't happen. That's your slobber."

"Now who's lying? I'm going to check the tub since I'm up." He disappeared into the bathroom and was back in a flash, his bobbing erection looking a bit painful. "We have time."

"From the way you look, you won't need much time."

He grinned. "No, I won't. And I want no complaints since you just came twice."

She lifted both hands in surrender, the solid gold band on her left ring finger catching her attention briefly. "Fine. No complaints. For now."

He climbed back on the bed, considering it and her for a few seconds. Then his grin widened. "How does my little sadist want me?"

"Flat on your back. In a starfish. I'm not tying you up but I want you to pretend you are. That means, unless I instruct you to move, don't."

She moved out of the way, and let him spread out as requested, not a complaint to be heard. He stretched his long arms and legs until his hands and feet were almost touching each corner of the king-sized bed. His erection was lying on his hip, a thick string of precum connecting the tip to the ridge of muscle there.

When she leaned over and quickly licked it away, he jerked. She lifted her head. "Don't move."

"That was involuntary."

"Mmm hmm."

She reached under the pillows and pulled out the chain first. His eyes focused on that and a flush rose up from his chest onto his throat, where she could see his pulse begin to pound.

Oh yes. It had been a long time since they'd used it and his reaction showed her that they needed to use it more often, just like the gel.

He said nothing, but his body went electric as she hooked the clamps to the small gold rings. The chain was long enough she could use them as reins.

She awkwardly straddled his waist, the head of his cock pressing against one of her ass cheeks, the slippery beads of fluid from the crown smearing against her skin.

This time when she reached under the pillow, she pulled out the feather. She twirled it within her fingers right in front of his face. His eyes went wide for only a split moment, then narrowed. But still, he said nothing.

He liked it rough. She liked it rough.

A feather was not rough. It was torture.

She brushed the feather over her closed lips, her chin, her neck, her chest and circled each nipple. After making sure her nipples were nice and peaked again, she continued over her rounded belly, past her pussy until she reached him.

His stomach lurched slightly when she lightly touched him.

"Don't move," she reminded firmly.

"Pull the chain." He wasn't asking...

"When I'm ready."

"Leah..."

She touched the feather to his lips. "Hush."

He hushed.

She started where she straddled him and slid the long, soft feather up over his six-pack—yes, he still had one at forty-one, just not as distinct as when she first met him—and she took her time, teasing his pierced and chained nipples lightly with the very tip.

"Leah," he groaned, his muscles tightening. A sign he was struggling to obey her orders of not moving.

"Hmm?"

She didn't expect an answer and didn't get one because he knew better than to complain. Complaining only extended the torture. The torture in this moment, being the soft touch of a feather.

She swept it down both sides of his face, along his nose, over his lips again, which were now parted as he panted slightly.

The precum was leaking steadily against the skin of her ass, where his cock was pressed. He also kept flexing it against her, giving her an indication of just how hard he was.

Which meant he was ready to explode.

"Stay there," she whispered, with a last brush of the ostrich feather over his chest, nipples and stomach. Then she carefully climbed off of him and the bed, and headed into the bathroom to check the tub.

"Leah!" he shouted.

She smiled as she turned off the water since it was over the level it needed to be for two people. Water would be spilled but it would be worth it.

Now they needed to hurry up before it turned cold.

But she didn't hurry, she took her time. Before she stepped out of the bathroom she said, "You better not have moved. I have a photographic memory."

"I would know if you did!" he shouted, sounding very frustrated.

"I just never told you because I was waiting for the right moment." She stepped out of the bathroom and looked at the bed. "And now it is..." She gasped dramatically. "You moved!"

"No, I didn't!"

"No nipple play for you," she scolded as she went back to the bed.

"Leah," he groaned.

She climbed back over him, staying on her knees so her wet pussy didn't touch his skin. She scooched back just enough to hover over his cock, then lowered herself to slide her slick folds along his length.

"Fuck... Leah... please..."

His face was flush, his eyes dark and unfocused, his body slightly trembling.

"Well, since you said 'please'..." She picked the chain off his chest and held it within her fingers, but not pulling, which was what he wanted. She scraped her fingernail over the tips of both nipples, pulling a groan from him. Lifting her hips again, she reached down to grab his pulsing cock, and adjusted herself until the slick head of it was tucked right between her folds. She slid the crown back and forth a couple times, his eyes fluttering closed and his jaw getting tight.

In one combined motion, she yanked hard on the chain at the same time she sank down. His back arched away from the bed, but he managed to keep his legs and arms in the starfish pose, where she told him to keep them.

She was impressed he could do it.

She continued to pull on the chain, the gold hoops stretching his nipples to the point they couldn't stretch anymore. He groaned again, even louder, his head rolling back and his hips pressing upward, driving himself deeper inside her.

"Oh fuck... I'm going to come."

She yanked harder on the chain—knowing his flesh wouldn't rip, but still always worried it would—and rode his cock, taking her time, rising and falling in a leisurely manner, knowing he'd prefer her pace to be much quicker.

"Leah." Her name turned into a low moan. "I'm going to come."

"Wait for me."

"I need to come," he begged.

"Wait for me," she said again, softly.

"I can't."

"Yes, you can. When I tell you, you can come deep inside me."

"Yes," he hissed, lifting his head off the pillow. "I need that."

She did, too.

"How soon?"

"Hush!"

He slammed his head back into the pillow and released a growl.

Dropping the chain, she leaned forward, unhooked it and tossed it aside, making him whimper. Planting her hands on his chest, she snagged both nipple rings between her thumbs and forefingers and twisted as hard as she could. His head, as well as his hips, shot up again, the tendons in his neck straining scarily, almost knocking her off balance. She managed to stay with him and began to ride him faster.

She wanted to come a third time.

"Oh fuck," he forced between gritted teeth, his eyes rolling back and his hips following an opposite direction than hers. When she rose, he'd drop his hips. Until she finally slammed down hard on him, grinding in a circle and her orgasm peaking and tumbling down around her, dragging her with it.

"Come," she cried out.

He grunted and slammed up into her, holding his hips off the bed, his cock pulsing inside her as he came.

She had closed her eyes during the pinnacle, but after a few moments she opened them, seeing complete satisfaction covering her husband's face. She released his nipples and kept her balance with her hands on his chest when he lowered himself back to the bed.

Without permission, he moved, quickly wrapping his arms around her and rolling her over until he was nose to nose with her. He whispered, "I fucking love you."

She smiled, brushing her fingers along the damp, short dark hairs on the side of his head. "You should after that."

"We need them to watch the kids more often."

He would get no argument about that from her. "Agreed."

"We also need to get in the Jacuzzi before the water turns cold. It'll be nice to soak my muscles while I recover and can fuck you again. This time with me in control."

"I also agree with those statements."

He brushed a kiss over her lips. "I can't ever get enough of you."

"I love you, Marc."

"I know. I feel and see it every day. I've got the best life, baby. I've got no complaints."

"Unless a dog's licking your balls."

"Or shitting in my shoes."

"Or one of the boys vomits in your lap."

He wrinkled his nose. "Or has stuff coming out of both ends at the same time." He made a gagging sound.

"Okay, I'm done with this game."

He pressed a light kiss on the tip of her nose. "Me fucking, too."

Marc rolled off the bed and held his hand out to Leah. She took it and groaned as he helped her to her feet, escorted her into the bathroom and turned on the jets in the full tub.

He kept a firm grip on her hand as she climbed in, not wanting her to slip, then followed her into the warm water. Before he sat down, he leaned past her and pulled up the blinds that covered the large picture window overlooking the back of their small tree farm.

She saw it at the same time he did. "*Ohhhh.* It's snowing! So perfect for Christmas Eve."

He grimaced and, with a last glance outside at the snow-covered yard and the rows of Christmas trees beyond, settled across from her in the two-person Jacuzzi. "That might make for a messy parade route today."

"It makes it feel more like Christmas."

He didn't mind snow if he didn't have to work. Or his wife didn't have to work. Or his boys didn't have to get into a vehicle, which they did today. "That mountain of presents we bought them, as well as the rest of the family bought them, will no doubt make it feel like Christmas."

"But it makes the evergreens really pretty and the kids will love it."

Not only did their small farm butt up next to his parent's larger farm, his father had planted more evergreens on their property to expand their Christmas tree business. It was one of the reasons Marc bought the place.

Though, he had to completely redo the original farmhouse before he moved in over ten years ago.

He loved the property. It was peaceful. They had a clear view of the mountain range to the north and with their place being right next to his parents', his father kept the boys involved with the tree farm. They even sometimes hung out with Oliver at the Boneyard Bakery, while Amanda made the organic dog treats she shipped all over the world.

Having all three boys close in age was perfect, with Austin being six, cousin Oliver being five, and their current youngest, Jax, being four.

Yeah, they got into tussles but they got over their little spats quickly. Plus, his pop had no qualms in taking any of the boys by the collar and getting them straightened out. Not only was the man a great father but he was an unbelievable grandfather and lived for his grandkids.

Marc couldn't ask for more.

Except for baby number three to be a girl. For Leah. She wanted another girl in the house badly and he wanted it for her.

Plus, Hannah was Max's "Daddy's Little Girl" and Marc kind of wanted that for himself. But no matter what the baby was, as long as he or she was happy and healthy, they'd be happy.

They had chosen to find out what they were having when Leah was pregnant with Austin and Jax, but this time, they decided they wanted to be surprised.

It was hard waiting. He had to stop from asking Carly, who was Leah's OB/GYN, just about every time he saw her. Which was a lot. If he cheated and found out behind Leah's back... And then she discovered he knew? He winced. She would tear his piercings right out of his nipples.

"You're too far away." Leah's voice pulled him from his thoughts.

"The tub isn't that big, Leah. It's not an Olympic-sized pool. And I have a reason for sitting here."

"What's that?"

He pulled his hand from the bubbling water and held his palm out flat. "I'm starting your Christmas gift early."

She tilted her head and stared at his hand, confused.

"I got you, Mom, Carly and Amanda a full day at the spa. A whole day of pampering for the women in my life."

"What?" she whispered. She fluttered her eyelashes and shuddered. "I think I just came again."

He laughed. "I figured you'd like that. I know how uncomfortable you get and maybe this will help just a little, since you insist you only got pregnant again for me."

"And why are you holding your hand like that?"

"Because, like I said, I'm going to start it early."

She looked at him suspiciously. "What?"

He rolled his eyes. "Give me your foot."

Her frown was quickly replaced with a soft smile and as her leg rose from the water, he grabbed it, sliding both hands down her smooth calf, around her ankle and to her foot. The second he wrapped his fingers around it, she groaned.

"I didn't even do anything yet."

"I know," she breathed, "but..."

He held her heel with one hand and began to use the magic fingers of his other on the sole of her foot, between her toes, in the arch, along the top...

Her moans and groans were music to his ears. The harder he pressed, the louder she got. She leaned her head back against the edge of the tub, closed her eyes and her body turned to putty right before his.

"Marc."

He grinned at the liquid way she said his name. "Yeah, baby?"

"You're a god right now."

He chuckled. "I finally achieved my life's goal."

"Just. Don't. Stop."

"I'm not stopping until you tell me to."

She lifted one eyelid. "Well, then they might have to bury us together in this tub because I'm never telling you to stop."

"Okay, I'll stop once I get hard again."

The other eyelid opened. "You *are* getting older, so that might be a while."

"The way you're moaning and groaning? It might be just a few minutes."

"Then keep massaging. You need to do both feet equally before that happens."

She closed her eyes, leaned her head back again and let out a long sigh as he continued to rub and work the tension out of her feet.

He'd never been a foot man, but he'd have to admit that his

wife's were pretty damn sexy. Perfectly shaped and well-manicured, with the toenails painted a feminine lavender. Purple was her favorite color.

He lifted her foot higher, careful not to upset her balance and kissed along the bottom of her foot.

"Marc..."

He sucked her big toe into his mouth.

Both eyes popped open. "Marc!"

"You don't like that?"

"Stick to your hands, not your mouth, please."

He grinned and teased her by slipping his tongue between two of her toes and waggling it.

"Marc! That's probably what it felt like when Trouble licked your balls!"

"Fine, if you don't appreciate my tongue."

"Believe me, I appreciate it, just not there. Rub."

"Slave driver," he grumbled.

Her other foot nudged between his thighs and her toes pressed gently against his sac.

"What are you doing?"

"Just seeing how much time I have left before you're hard."

"If you keep toeing my balls, you're going to run out of time before I get to that foot."

She jerked the foot he was holding out of his grip so quickly water splashed him right in the eye.

"Hey!"

"Here, do this one quick." She shoved the foot that had been between his legs into his chest. "Rub."

"Woman, do you know how bossy you sound?"

"You like it."

"Not when it's my turn. You got your chance in there to take control. Now it's all me."

"Okay. Please?"

His lips curled up at the ends as he let his gaze roam over her dark brown hair and her brown eyes, which were crinkled at the corners as she grinned.

Just as fucking beautiful as the first day he saw her in Max's office at Manning Grove PD in her ill-fitted Kevlar vest.

His rookie.

He had no idea just how much his life would change by being forced to become her Field Training Officer. Max had crowed in delight at sticking him with the job since, at the time, Marc didn't believe women belonged in law enforcement.

Max proved him wrong.

So did Leah.

And he'd gotten back at Max by getting involved with the Chief's newest recruit and giving his older brother heartburn a few times.

In the end, it all worked out. Thank fuck for that.

The PD got a great cop, Marc got the best wife, and the Bryson family got a new female member. Like Leah, his mother hoped for at least one girl. She never got it and wouldn't risk having a fourth child in case she got stuck with four boys. But she did finally get the daughters she desired once Amanda, Leah and Carly came into their lives.

And Teddy, of course.

He snorted and massaged Leah's foot more intently, drawing little whimpers from her that did not discourage his cock coming back into action.

Now his mom also had Hannah. Marc not only wanted Leah to get her girl, but his mother, too. Max and Amanda were done with two kids. He and Leah were done after this one. And Carly and Matt recently adopted a boy.

That meant the baby Leah was carrying was Ron and Mary Ann's last opportunity at a second granddaughter.

Marc pulled on her ankle gently. "C'mere, baby."

Leah's brown eyes opened and her face got soft. She loved

when he called her that. He didn't do it often to keep it special for her.

And he was afraid of slipping while they were on duty and calling her that in front of their fellow officers.

When she shifted in the tub, more water splashed over the side. Normally, they would care but at that moment, neither did. This time was for them.

Just husband and wife. Lovers reconnecting.

He grabbed her hand, turned her around and settled her body between his legs, so she could lean back against his chest. He pressed his cheek to hers and circled his arms around her, planting his hands firmly on her growing belly.

He spread his fingers and murmured, "It's a girl. I just know it."

"I love that you want that for me, Marc. And while I want it, too, I'm trying not to get my hopes up. Your mom had three boys, so our odds aren't good."

"Can you live with three boys?"

"Do I have a choice?"

He pressed a kiss to her cheek. "Well, you could run away."

She reached back and spread her fingers across his cheek as he began to rub her stomach. She sighed and relaxed against him. "As long as it's yours, I'll be happy with whatever it is."

"Liar."

"Wait. Which part am I lying about?"

"I know that kid's mine."

"Are you sure?" she asked.

"I'm irresistible, remember? You haven't looked at another man since the second you saw me."

Leah made a choking sound. "If you didn't know, you really don't have to *look* at a man to get pregnant by him."

"Oh, were you visiting some glory holes?"

She shook against him. "Only one was needed, apparently," she said as she placed her hand over his as he continued to make wide circles over her belly.

He loved when she was pregnant. Even two kids later, he was fascinated at the fact she was capable of growing and carrying another life inside her. A life that they created together.

Under the water, she ran her fingers back and forth from his knees to his thighs. His hands shifted higher to the top curve of her belly, his knuckles brushing the undersides of her heavy breasts.

Oh hell yes, he loved when she was pregnant. And breastfeeding.

She turned her head enough to offer her mouth, so he took it, sliding his tongue inside to taste and tangle with hers.

The power shift they had even happened with kissing. One second he would be ravishing her mouth, the next, she would do it to him.

She reminded him constantly in the littlest ways that she was an equal. And just because she could bear children, didn't mean she was only a mother.

She was so much more.

And, lucky bastard that he was, she was also his.

The woman in his arms was intelligent, strong and highly driven. That made her sexy as fuck. The bigger boobs during pregnancy didn't hurt, either. Though, he kept that lecherous thought to himself since he liked his nuts right where they currently hung.

He pulled his tongue back and she chased it with hers into his mouth, taking control of the kiss, deepening it and adding the vibration of her groan to the mix.

He cupped the undersides of her breasts, squeezing gently, while thumbing the nipples, the tips turning into tight nubs. He captured and twisted them between his fingers, causing her to release another long groan into his mouth, encouraging him to continue. He turned the gentle motion into a more demanding one, twisting harder and faster. She ground her ass back into his balls and his now semi-erect cock.

He broke the kiss, pushed her partially wet hair away from her neck and nibbled at the skin where it met her shoulder.

"Look at you, rising to the occasion a lot quicker than expected." Her voice was throaty, exactly how it got when she was turned on and ready to ride her husband.

"Well, my wife called me a god, so..."

She dropped her head and shook against him again, her ass wiggling into his crotch, which encouraged his cock to grow even more.

"Did you bring in that cock ring?" she asked.

"Of course, I get off on those vibrations just as much as you."

She reached behind her and patted his cheek. "I know you do. It's a conundrum. The ring keeps you hard while those vibrations make you want to blow."

"Mmm," he murmured, kissing along the damp curve of her shoulder. "*You* make me want to blow."

"Better put it on now before you get too hard." She twisted. "Or let me."

"I'll do it. Last time you just about neutered me."

"Well, you shouldn't have moved so much!"

"I was trying to escape your sadistic torture. You had me trapped by my dick."

"It's a very nice dick."

"That should remain attached if you want to continue to use it."

"Fine, then. You put it on."

He grabbed the ring from the edge of the tub behind him, and, under the water, worked it down his ever-growing cock. "Do you want the thingy at the top or the bottom."

She tilted her head as if in deep thought. "I want to face you."

He adjusted the ring until the vibrating part was at the top, where it would press against her clit. They hadn't used it in a while but the last time they did, she had multiple explosive orgasms. They had no choice but to change the sheets afterward.

He hoped this morning brought about the same.

"Get ready for a tsunami. In and out of the tub," she warned him. "We might have to get out the Shop-Vac to suck up all the water on the floor."

"I'm okay with that."

She turned to face him. "Which means, I'll be doing the cleanup."

"I have to work, remember? I wasn't lucky enough to get off today."

She grabbed his chin and reminded him, "Oh, you'll be getting off."

He grinned.

She grinned.

"Climb on my cock, wife."

She tried to keep a straight face as she moved to straddle his lap. She reached between them and turned on the vibration. As soon as she did, he groaned as his cock began to hum and his balls pulled tight immediately.

Damn. Even though he already shot a load earlier, he might not last long this time, either. "Turn down the speed," he managed to get out between clenched teeth.

Her fingers played around the ring that snuggly circled the root of his cock and the vibrations slowed down a little. He hoped that helped.

"Leah, get on." Unfortunately, that sounded more frantic than he'd like, but she needed to move quickly.

She planted her hands on his shoulder and once again reached down, holding him in place. *Christ,* just that alone caused the pressure to build to a dangerous level.

"Ready?" she whispered. A smile ghosted across her face.

"I can see you are."

"I can see you are, too." *Oh yeah,* his cock was definitely ready for action again.

She slid the head of it between her folds once, tucked it where it needed to be and tortured him by *slowly* lowering herself.

"Leah," he breathed. "*Fuck*... Hurry."

She took his whole length, paused, then ground down until her clit rode the vibrator part while her pussy swallowed his cock.

Fuck.

Fuck.

Fuck.

Now he remembered why they didn't use it often. Sex would only last seconds.

He choked out, "Leah," in a warning.

"Holy shit," she breathed, grinding against him, which was not helping his predicament.

"Holy shit is right and you're going to be pissed if I come before you."

She pressed her lips to his ear. "Pissed doesn't even come close. You better not come before I tell you."

"No, we're not playing that game. The power is supposed to be mine right now."

"Then take it."

"Hard to take it when you're on top."

"Bullshit," she groaned.

"Okay, then..." He reached behind her head, grabbed a handful of her wet hair and pulled it so hard, her head snapped back, exposing her throat. He ignored her gasp, and sank his teeth into her delicate flesh there and sucked the skin. He had to be careful about leaving marks since they were spending time with his family the next two days and didn't need his ass ridden about it.

He scraped his teeth down the side of her neck and to her shoulder. Now *there* he could leave a mark no one but him would see. If he left a mark there, every time he'd see it in the next couple days, he'd get hard as a rock. *Hell,* all he would have to do is think about it and *BAM!*

Being in his forties hadn't slowed his sexual prowess down at all. He'd have to make sure to rub that in.

When he could speak.

She cried out as he bit the flesh of her shoulder, and her pussy squeezed around him as she rode him faster and ground against him harder. She dug her short nails into his back, also doing her best to leave marks.

Fuck yes.

Seeing scratches on his back would get him worked up, too.

Placing his lips over his bite, he sucked until he knew he pulled the blood to the surface, sure to leave his mark on her.

He pictured her now, naked in front of the bathroom mirror, running her fingers over that mark, her pussy twinging and becoming wet. She would slide her finger through her arousal, come find him and slip her finger into his mouth.

When she did that, it got him instantly hard.

And right now, the thought of that happening in a day or two, sent any blood left, already not in his cock, right to it, making him painfully hard.

"Leah," he murmured against her skin.

"I'm going to come." Her voice sounded strained since her neck was still arched back as far as it would go.

"That's the point," he ground out, trying his best to hold on. He was quickly failing as she ground her clit hard against the top part of the cock ring. "Leah," he whimpered.

Yes, whimpered.

"I'm going to," she groaned, "come."

So was he.

He snagged one of her nipples between his fingers, pinching it so hard, she jerked against him.

The wail she released at the same time as her pussy contracted around him, made him shove his face into her neck and groan, "Oh God, baby," as he surged up and came so hard his cock pulsed like it had its own heart.

They both remained still as their bodies convulsed, and when they stopped, he released her hair, she lifted her head and gave him a lazy smile.

She then fell against him, her muscles limp, her arms around his neck and her cheek pressed to his. "We need to use that ring whenever we can only get in a quickie."

"It definitely turns sex into a quickie."

"That means we'll be able to fit more in."

He jerked his head back and stared at her. "You want more quickies?"

"I want more sex in general. I just know it's not realistic with our different shifts, the boys and then," she placed her hand on her belly, "a new baby on the way. But really, Marc, I love having sex with you and it's a good time for us to connect and forget about having to adult."

"Um, okay. Count me in for more quickies."

She laughed. "I didn't think you'd say no."

"If I ever do, you better take me to get examined."

"I love you. I know our life is hectic and it's just a good time to slow down."

"Quickies aren't slowing down," he reminded her.

"I know, but it's better than nothing."

"I— Uh. Oh fuck!" Marc stared beyond Leah and out the window. "Oh motherfuck!"

"What?" Leah twisted her head and whispered, "Oh shit. They can see us."

"Of course they can," he whispered back.

"Why are we whispering? They can't hear us."

"Don't move. Maybe they won't notice us."

"Marc, I'm sitting on your dick, we're both naked and—"

"I'm in the tub with you, Leah, I'm well aware of our status. Except... Okay, you're no longer sitting on my dick." He quickly reached between them, turned off the vibration and yanked the silicone cock ring off in a panic. He winced when it caught his delicate skin. He dropped it to the bottom of the tub. "Move very slowly and keep your boobs under the water."

"Well, yeah, I don't need to show an audience my breasts."

"I'm sure Pop wouldn't mind, but—"

She slowly shifted off his lap and to his side, sinking lower into the water.

They both remained frozen as his parents, the kids and Greg wandered the back edge of their yard along the tree line.

"Close the blinds."

"I have to stand up to do that," Marc hissed. "If I do, I'm going to flash my mother and Hannah. I'd prefer not to have to pay for my niece's therapy visits for the rest of her life."

"Your cock isn't *that* big and scary."

"Just pretend they're not there and stay still. Movement might catch their eye."

"You think?" she hissed. "Who puts such a big window in front of a tub?"

"Someone who was a bachelor and planned to remain that way and didn't think trespassers would be marching through his property while he was having sex in said tub."

"Well, you didn't plan that out well. Why'd they wait this long to put up a tree? They never do. They usually put it up Thanksgiving weekend."

Marc caught himself before he shrugged. "They wanted the kids to pick one out and help decorate it. I guess it was an activity to keep them busy before and after the parade today."

"There are five million Christmas trees on their property. Why are they searching over here?"

Good question. One he couldn't answer. "Oh shit," he groaned. "Did you move?"

Of course, the person they didn't want to spot them, did. "Hi!" The muffled shout could barely be heard as Greg waved at them. Everyone else's heads turned toward them, still naked in the tub.

Fuck.

"Damn. We're busted," Leah whispered.

"Hi!" Greg screamed again when neither responded. He loped across the yard and up to the window. "Hi, Marc! Hi, Lee!" He waved again. "Do you stink? Are... are you taking a bath?"

"Yes, we're just getting ready for the parade," Leah explained loudly, so Greg could hear her through the double-paned window.

Greg bounced on his toes and wrung his hands together. "The parade! Max is in the parade!"

"Yeah, buddy, he is," Marc answered. "I think Grandpa is trying to get your attention."

Once Hannah began calling Ron Grandpa, Greg asked if he could call him Grandpa, too, along with calling Mary Ann, "Gramma." And, of course, they were thrilled. Marc's mother even shed a few tears at the request.

Greg ignored Ron's shout. Then his father said something to his mother, who gathered the rest of the children and disappeared into a row of trees.

At least his mother listened.

Unlike Greg, who was oblivious to the situation.

"It's snowing!" Greg yelled, his hands flapping with excitement and his eyes rolling. A huge smile covered his face. The man loved snow and he was the only one since he didn't have to drive or work in it.

"Yeah, buddy, it is. Grandpa needs you to help pick out a tree."

"Greg, go with Grandpa," Leah encouraged.

"Are you taking a bath together?" Greg asked.

Marc's eyes met his father's amused ones as he strode across the snow-covered lawn toward them.

"Oh shit," he muttered under his breath.

"Hey, Dad," Leah greeted weakly as Ron stepped up to the window, not hiding his grin.

"Getting cleaned up?"

"Yep," Marc answered his pop.

"Conserving water there, I see."

"Yep," Marc repeated.

"The environment will now be saved," his father said with a nod. "We can all breathe a little easier."

"Pop," Marc ground out.

Ron turned his head and put a hand to his ear. "Sorry, what? Hard to hear you through the window in front of your Jacuzzi tub, even though those blinds are wide open."

"Wasn't expecting you to do your own little parade through the property today."

Ron cocked an eyebrow. "Apparently."

"Wasn't this what your and Mom's Christmas gift was about?"

His father pursed his lips. "Was it?"

"Pop!"

Ron chuckled. "It was to give you all a break from the kids. I'm glad you're taking full advantage of it." He turned to Greg and grabbed the younger man's shoulder. "Let's go, Greg, before the kids pick out a lopsided tree. We can't have that."

"Can't have that," Greg parroted. He shot a last wave at them through the window. "Bye! Bye, Marc! Bye, Lee!"

"Bye, Greg," they both answered at the same time.

"See you at the parade!" Greg shouted as Ron escorted him away with a firm grip on his shoulder.

Once they both disappeared into the trees, both Marc and Leah breathed easier.

"Hurry up and close the blinds so we can get out." Leah glanced around. "Where's the cock ring?"

"I dropped it in the water." He stood up, the water sluicing off him, and pulled the blinds.

"Oh, thank goodness! I had this nightmare of Ron seeing it sitting on the edge of the tub."

"Me, too. And that would be my luck. Open the drain." He climbed out of the tub and held out his hand to her to help her out. "I'll grab the wet vac since we flooded the bathroom."

"And while you do that, I'll make you breakfast. What do you want?" She stepped out of the tub and he held onto her since the tiles were wet.

"You. Across the kitchen table."

She paused in front of him, tapping his cheek. "You're very ambitious today."

He dropped his head until their lips were almost touching. "Trying to make the most out of the time we were given."

"I appreciate that, but your kid needs food."

He released a dramatic huff. "Fine. We'll eat first and then if we have time, I'll take you on the kitchen table."

"Or I'll take you." She said, giving him a quick kiss and pulling away.

He grabbed her wrist and stopped her from leaving the bathroom. "Hey."

She paused and glanced over her shoulder. "What?"

"Thank you for putting up with me."

She stared at him for the longest time, her face unreadable.

"And my family," he quickly added.

"I only put up with you because you come with them," she teased. Her face went soft. "But they're my family, too. I can't imagine life without them."

"I could."

She laughed and he watched his beautiful, naked, pregnant wife walk out the door.

CHAPTER THREE

MATT & CARLY

arly turned over and her hand went out.

Nothing.

Matt's side of the bed was empty. *Shit.*

She shot up in bed, willing her eyes to focus.

Had he had a nightmare again and disappeared?

Her gaze landed on his cell phone on the nightstand. *Shit.*

She couldn't even ping his location. He wasn't supposed to go anywhere without it. He had agreed to that. This way if he went into a dark headspace, she'd at least know where he was and if he was safe. She'd have some way to track him down. Or have a location to send one of his brothers to find him.

They had agreed.

Especially after he'd disappeared when they first lived together. When he had checked himself into a mental health facility for a month without a word.

He'd been so good about keeping his phone with him. She hoped he wasn't slipping.

Not now, not when...

She glanced at the digital clock. 4:02.

She'd been up half the night because Levi had been fussy. She listened carefully and didn't hear a baby crying or a man moving around the house.

It was too quiet. But then their bedroom door was closed. She never closed it so they could hear Levi in the room directly across the hall.

She shoved the covers off and slid out of bed. She padded barefoot across the room, out of the bedroom and was surprised to find the nursery's door closed. Had she closed it automatically in her exhaustion?

She quietly opened the door and peeked into the dark room only lit by a nightlight. It was bright enough that she could see them perfectly.

Her husband sitting in the rocking chair, holding Levi against his broad chest, giving the baby a bottle. His head was dipped down and he was talking in a low, soothing voice...

Telling Levi a story Matt was making up as he went.

Her heart swelled and she put her hand over her mouth as the first tear slipped from the corner of her eye. She didn't want to disturb them, but she couldn't not watch the two bonding.

Father and son.

Levi had downy hair, as dark as Matt's, and right now had blue eyes. Hopefully they would remain blue, just like his birth mother's. Just like Matt's.

She wiped away another tear that ran down her face. She had worried about him, but she had no reason to. He had stepped in to take care of Levi without her asking.

To Matt, having a baby didn't come naturally and he had to work at it. But he was willing. He was willing to do whatever he needed to do to give her her dream of having a child.

And that right there caused another tear to fall.

His deep, smooth voice tapered off and he continued to stare at Levi for what seemed like minutes, when it was probably seconds. Lifting his head, he spotted Carly standing in the doorway.

"He was fussy again," Matt whispered, carefully rising to his feet, the baby tucked in one arm, the empty bottle in his other hand.

He placed the bottle on the changing table, carefully moved a sleeping Levi to his shoulder where he had a towel draped over it and gently patted the baby's back until he let out the smallest burp. Matt grinned and laid Levi in his crib on his back.

"Does he need to be changed first?"

Matt stared into the crib and murmured, "Already done." He nodded, like he was assuring himself that Levi was fine and he could leave him. With a last look, he turned and approached her, still stuck in the doorway.

"You could've woken me up. You have to work today, I don't," she reminded him.

"I know. But I wanted to help. He's my son, too."

Oh yes, he certainly was.

Jesus. She couldn't stop crying. He wiped a tear off her cheek with his thumb.

She dropped her forehead to his chest and his arms automatically came around her. "God, Matt. I got scared when I woke up and you weren't in bed."

"I didn't take my phone."

"I know."

"We have an agreement that if I leave the house, I take my phone."

"I know."

"I wanted you to get some sleep. You've been up most of the night."

Her third "I know," never quite made it past her lips since a sob beat it. He kissed her forehead and wrapped his fingers around the back of her neck.

"C'mon," he urged, steering her around with the grip on her neck and back across the hall, leaving Levi's door partially open.

He left their door only open a crack. She normally liked it

wider than that and when she went to push it open, he snagged her wrist and stopped her.

"Leave it for now."

She flicked her eyes up to his face and noticed how his eyes had darkened and his nostrils flared. That was one way to get rid of her tears.

"What do you want, Marine?" she whispered.

"My wife." He grabbed her hand and pressed it to his erection under his boxers, proving what he said was true.

She pinned her lips together so she wouldn't smile. "You're assuming your wife wants you right now at zero dark thirty after a couple hours of sleep at most."

He lifted one dark eyebrow. "Does she not?"

"She might be able to drum up some enthusiasm," she teased, sliding her fingers over the long, hard ridge. "Especially since you're already at attention."

He grinned and thumbed her nipples through the long-sleeved cotton nightshirt she slept in. The one that said, "Lay down the law, do a cop," across the chest. He had bought it for her last Christmas as a joke. But she wore it all last winter and had dug it out again this year once it got cold.

She supposed it was fitting since she was about to "do a cop."

The brush of his thumbs made her nipples turn to tight nubs, then he pinched the tips gently.

"Stay right where you are," she ordered, walking past him toward the bed, pulling off the nightshirt as she went.

"Yes, Ma'am," he answered.

She tossed it onto the nearby chair, knowing it would drive him crazy that she'd thrown it haphazardly. She slipped out of her panties and threw those on top, too, then turned to face him after rethinking climbing onto the bed. That could wait.

He had plans. Well, so did she.

She saw where his head had turned and noticed his shoulders had tensed. "My clothes are on the chair. What's more important? That they aren't folded, or that your wife is currently naked?"

Having a child would test his Post-Traumatic Stress-induced Obsessive-Compulsive Disorder, so she was trying to work with him to let the less important things go.

A child was never going to be neat and orderly. Toys, clothes, food... Levi would create plenty of messes. He also wouldn't understand that his father would struggle when seeing them.

"Now, get undressed and keep your back toward me. Your wife wants to inspect her Marine."

She could imagine his grin at her words. His shoulders loosened and he crossed his arms over his abdomen, grabbed the bottom of his worn, loose olive drab T-shirt and slowly pulled it up his torso and over his head.

Without hesitation, he also dropped his drawers.

She let her gaze roam over him from his high and tight hair style, his corded neck, across his broad shoulders. It touched on the large Marines logo inked in black and grey into his back, the American Flag, and the words *Semper Fi* in a banner beneath it.

One thing her husband was, was loyal.

Dedicated to a fault.

The round globes of his muscular ass drew her attention next. He worked out like a fiend. Alternating running and weights, keeping his body sculpted like an Adonis. Unlike her, who was a bit soft around the middle.

But he needed to expel his anxiety somehow and going for a long run sometimes helped. Because of his routine, his thighs were powerful, his calves perfectly formed.

"Turn around." She whispered the order, but he heard it. He was listening carefully for her commands.

He slowly turned and the first thing she noticed was his cock in his hand. The second was the raised scar along his ribs where he took a piece of shrapnel during one of his tours.

Proof he could have died serving his country. Carly couldn't imagine never having met him and loved him, or helping him through his struggles.

The years he dedicated to the Marines left him a broken man. And once the Corps discovered just how broken he was, they sent him home against his will. He had felt betrayed after the years of loyalty, years of his life, he'd given. His heart hadn't been ready to go, but his mind was too messed up to stay.

The Marine Corps gave him up damaged and Carly accepted him as-is.

Every day was a journey and some were more difficult than others. But the good days were worth dealing with the bad. And the man standing before her was worth it.

"Looking mighty edible there, Marine."

"Yes, Ma'am," he barked softly.

Her lips curved in a slight smile as he folded both the T-shirt and boxers before stacking them neatly on the dresser. He probably would never be able to break that habit with his own stuff.

She accepted it.

It was who he was.

That was Matt.

And the OCD was the least of his issues.

While his meds helped, his career as a cop did, too, especially since he worked with people, like his brothers, who knew what he dealt with. His family was also very supportive, even in his darkest moments.

He rarely had those anymore but they still sometimes simmered just beneath the surface.

Waiting.

Just waiting for a reason to reappear.

She worried that bringing Levi home would upset his current calm. Babies were exhausting and could be frustrating, especially when they were crying or screaming and no one could figure out why.

In the five weeks since they brought Levi home from the hospital, Matt had adjusted better than expected. And luckily, Levi had done well, too. Especially after the circumstances surrounding his conception, pregnancy and birth.

Levi was a fighter, just like his birth mother, Autumn, and also like Matt.

For a man who had never wanted children...

He was already attached to their adopted son and she worried that if anything happened to Levi, he would shatter into so many pieces he'd never be able to put himself back together again.

Matt was the toughest man she knew.

He was also the most fragile.

She couldn't love anyone more than she did him.

Except for Levi.

Her two "men" had stolen her heart and soul.

She walked back to him, his eyes intense as they followed her. And when they stood toe to toe, she traced his lips lightly with her fingertips. His tongue darted out to touch them.

"I love you," she breathed.

For the longest time, her telling him that scared him. Even now, when she said it, she didn't miss the slight twinge.

It was a reaction he couldn't control.

She circled him, dragging her fingers from one shoulder, along his collarbones, to the other shoulder and then across the top of his back. She raked her nails lightly down his spine, pulling a shiver from him.

She stepped over to the wall because with what she wanted from him, she would need support. She placed her back against it and called his name softly, "Matt."

He glanced over his shoulder at where she stood, but he didn't move from near the dresser. She hadn't given him that instruction yet.

She could see the pulse pounding in his neck, and his chest now rose and fell more quickly.

Her own nipples ached for his touch, and she could feel her arousal dampening between her upper thighs.

"Matt. Front and center."

Every time she gave him an order and he obeyed without question, without hesitation and with complete trust, it made her own pulse race, her heart beat rapidly and her lose her breath.

She had been surprised to find it turned her on. Turned him on. But it was more than that...

"To your knees, Marine," she directed when he stepped close enough for her to feel his heat and the warm puffs of his ragged breathing.

He immediately dropped to his knees and bowed his head, lowering his gaze.

The man was beautiful. He had no problems putting himself in her hands completely. During sex, he actually preferred it. Needed it. It was when he could give up total control and let someone else dictate his actions. Like in the Marines, when he was given orders.

He got used to being told what to do and how to do it. It got him through his years of service, through the devastation he not only witnessed, but helped create.

Well, it had almost gotten him through, until everything became too much. Became too overwhelming to the point where he broke.

And had been broken ever since.

She lifted one bare foot and placed it on his right shoulder. He rose higher, but remained on his knees, as she dropped hers open, exposing herself to him. She brushed her hand over his hair and pushed on the back of his head. That was the only directive he needed.

He fell forward, his mouth latching onto her pussy, his tongue sliding through her folds before planting his lips on her clit and sucking.

She kept her ass pinned to the wall and let him do his thing, because he was good at it and needed no instructions.

Instead, she closed her eyes and breathed, enjoying his mouth on her. He knew when to use his lips, his tongue, his teeth. When to nibble, to lick, to suck, to flick.

He knew what would send her over the edge immediately, and what would draw out the pleasure.

"Stroke yourself," she managed to say.

She forced open her eyes to watch. Because, while her husband was beautiful, watching him stroke his thick erection turned him into a stunning work of art.

His fingers wrapped around the root, squeezed until the veins protruded, and when he began to fist himself, his mouth continued the onslaught on her pussy.

Her legs trembling, she pressed herself harder into the wall. Otherwise, she might slide down and melt into a puddle.

While sucking on her clit, he dragged two fingers through her folds, gathering her juices. Using that and the precum beading at the tip of his cock, he began to fist faster now that it was lubed.

The faster he stroked the faster he licked, pulling a shaky moan from between her lips. "Matt." The toes on the foot she had planted on his shoulder curled and she began to wobble dangerously, so she slammed one hand onto the wall and used the other to grab his head, holding on for balance.

Hot breath beat rapidly against her pussy.

"Don't you dare come," she ordered. "That's mine."

His stroking slowed, his mouth did not, and he made a noise. Whatever it was, was muffled. But she had a feeling he was struggling. Her muddled mind needed to remember that she ordered him to masturbate, that meant she needed to order him to stop.

"Stop stroking and make me come." Her order sounded weak, as she was struggling herself.

The flat of his tongue brushed over her clit. A few more flicks with the tip and a scrape of his teeth, and she was there.

Her fingers flexed against his head, her nails digging in. She slapped a hand over her mouth to smother the wail that rushed from her, and her orgasm made her buck against him. He held her hips, stabilizing her, holding her from simply dropping to the floor and he pulled his mouth away. From his place on his knees, he tipped his face up, his eyelids heavy, his light blue eyes unfocused, his lips shiny and parted.

A string of precum hung off the very tip of his cock.

"On your feet." Her words came out breathless and, again, not at all like the order she meant them to be, but he rose anyway, his eyes pinned to hers. "I want that."

And that's all she had to say. He caught the dangling string on his thumb and lifted it to her lips.

"Fuck," he groaned as she took his digit into her mouth and licked it clean.

"Another time," she answered his unspoken question. She didn't want to go to her knees, she wanted him to take her against the wall.

"I want to serve you."

That gruff statement sent a shudder through her. "You do."

"You know what I need."

"I do." Because she needed the same.

"Give me what I need." His raspy voice sending another shiver down her spine.

"Marine, your order this morning is to give me what I need."

He wasn't expecting that order. With only a slight hesitation, he grabbed her wrists, turned her and placed her palms flat on the wall, trapping her there. He didn't release her, instead he used his nose to nudge her long hair off her shoulder and away from her neck, his warm breath tickling her skin.

"Ma'am, yes, Ma'am," he finally whispered against the top of her spine, which made her pussy spasm once more.

He sucked at the base of her neck, then took little bites across each shoulder, causing her to moan. The small nips weren't painful, but it got her blood humming. He released her wrists when he licked down her spine... stopping right at the top of her crease and sucking the flesh there.

"Matt..."

His lips skimmed up the line of her spine as he rose and, when he did, he reached around and cupped her left breast with his right hand, while he hooked his left arm around her waist and slid his hand lower, until his fingertips brushed over her patch of hair, then teased her clit.

He kneed her legs wider, the same he would do if he was searching a subject. He hooked two fingers inside her and bent his knees just enough so the head of his cock brushed his own knuckles. He guided himself inside her.

His fingers found her clit again and his cock now filled her.

Yessss.

His powerful thighs flexed as he drove up and into her as his teeth pressed into the delicate flesh where her neck met her shoulder. Every thrust was accompanied with a deep grunt against her skin.

God, yes.

He circled her clit and twisted her nipple, not slowing down, giving it to her just how she needed it at that moment.

As twisted as Matt's mind could get, he was also very in tune with her. It surprised her time and time again. He could pick up on the littlest things. When she thought he was lost in his own head or had become withdrawn, he was still paying attention.

She had no idea how he did it. But when it came to the small details—as well as the big ones like sex—it made dealing with his issues a whole lot more bearable.

It was one reason Max had kept him on the force. Matt was good at reading people. He was good at his job. And he wasn't afraid of anything.

Plus, he was squared away to the extreme. She couldn't imagine he'd ever wear a uniform with the sleeve crease even slightly crooked.

No, she knew he wouldn't.

He ironed his uniforms himself. And he spent a lot of time making them perfect.

Everything had to be a particular way and everything in his life also had a place.

He was better now than when she first met him, not long after he was medically discharged from the Marines. But he'd never be the same young man who had joined, wanting to fight for his country, a country that hadn't always fought for him.

But Carly did. She would fight for him until the day she died.

However right now, she was ready for *la petite mort*, "the little death," as she bucked against him with each surge of his hips, each plunge of his cock, making her wetter, making him harder. She threw her head back against his shoulder, breaking the contact of his bite from her skin. He released her nipple and wrapped his fingers tightly around the front of her throat. Tight enough to remind her just how powerful he was. How it wouldn't take much for him to hurt her.

He never had.

He never would.

Though, he had feared plenty of times that he could.

He shoved his face into her neck and she swore she heard him beg, "Please."

He wanted to please her. And, in turn, she wanted to give him what he needed.

"Come with me, Marine," she commanded.

His grip tightened even more on her throat, allowing her to breathe but not move. Her knees wobbled as the pressure inside her began to build.

She was close. She clenched around his cock and he grunted.

"Come for me," he growled in her ear, surprising her with his unexpected demand.

He was now pounding her into the wall, his hips slapping against her ass in a quick rhythm.

"Come," she urged, "now."

He slammed deep one more time and stilled. As her climax rippled around him, he pumped cum deep inside her with a low groan.

Her name broke on his lips, and he pressed his chest against her back, pinning her against the wall.

He kissed her gently where he bit her, then rubbed his stubbled cheek along hers, trying to catch his breath. When it slowed, he gently slipped from her, turned her around and guided her to the bed.

"I need to clean up first," she whispered.

"No, not yet." The idea she held a piece of him inside her gave him a strange sense of peace.

In truth, it meant nothing. She already wore his wedding band on her finger. Just like she already had his last name. She hadn't argued it, she wanted to become a Bryson completely.

She had become a part of his family from the moment he saw her in the hospital that day, when she helped bring Hannah into the world.

Seeing her bark commands while Amanda was in labor, he had jokingly thought of her as the "dictator doctor." But in truth, her taking control of the situation caught his attention and made him want her.

But women hadn't been on his radar due to his issues, so he'd let it go until he couldn't ignore their connection.

He didn't want to burden her with those issues. But she was strong and hung in there with him. Even putting off her dream of adopting a baby and becoming a mother, just for him.

Just for him.

She did that for him.

He climbed into bed and rolled to his side, staring down into her face, meeting her soft, green eyes. His woman looked satisfied.

He was working the parade that afternoon and would be doing overtime so he could have Christmas day off to spend with his family. To spend with Levi on his first Christmas. So, he really needed to catch a few more zzz's, but right now, he needed to look at his wife and remind himself how lucky he was to have her.

She reached up and cupped his cheek. "You need more sleep. Are you working until eleven?"

"No, noon to eight to cover the parade and give some of the other officers who volunteered to work tomorrow a break."

"That was very kind of them to do so."

"They know how important tomorrow is."

"That gives me hope that this world will one day be more accepting in general."

He sighed and drew a knuckle down the soft skin of her cheek. He had caused her so much worry and pain the last few years. And adopting Levi was one of the ways he could show her his appreciation.

"Should I take Levi?" she asked.

"To the parade? Will he know what's going on?"

"Of course not, but—"

"It's too cold out for him."

He knew why Carly's lips twitched. The protective instinct that he had for Carly, he also had for his son. It had been instant. Holding the newborn right after he was born showed Matt how vulnerable Levi was.

"The whole family is gathering on the sidewalk in front of Manes on Main. Levi is the only grandchild not going over to your parents today to spend the day with them."

"Carly, he's five weeks old." There was no reason for Levi to be passed off to his parents today, they already had their hands full with the rest of the grandkids and Greg. Plus, the three of them were spending the next day at the farm, anyway.

"I'm aware of that, Matt. But he's a Bryson now and should be around his family."

Of course he should. But he didn't like the thought of Carly and Levi standing on the sidewalk, not only in the cold, but where a Shirley could spot them if they were skulking around. He also wasn't going to argue with her. One, he would lose and two, it would only get his blood pressure up. "Then take him. Teddy has a huge window in the salon. Just stand inside with him and watch the parade from there." At least they would be out of the elements and safer, which would give him some peace of mind.

Or at least he hoped so.

"I could do that."

"As long as I don't get a call, I'll be wandering around the parade route. I'll stop in and check on you two."

"That sounds like a plan."

He doubted any of the Shirleys would show up to watch the parade. They usually avoided town whenever possible. They hated the police. They hated the town council. They considered themselves a sovereign nation which governed themselves.

In reality, it was all bullshit. A sovereign nation wasn't recognized by the government, which meant they held no power and were subject to follow the same laws as everyone else.

But, unfortunately, those fuckwads didn't accept that. Which meant they were a thorn in the Manning Grove PD's side.

And even though his and Carly's names were on Levi's birth certificate and the baby bore the Bryson last name, Matt still worried about the Shirleys. That redneck clan on the mountain was unpredictable and their leader had raped Autumn repeatedly until she was pregnant with his child.

No matter what, that child wasn't a Shirley. He was a Bryson and Matt would protect him as such. At the parade, all the Brysons currently wearing a badge would be working and unable to watch Carly and Levi closely. The only one who would not be in uniform would be Leah, who was pregnant, and there was no way he'd risk anything happening to his unborn niece or nephew.

Having Leah still do patrol also freaked Matt the fuck out.

Why Marc put up with it, he didn't know. Matt had shared his displeasure with his chief, and oldest brother, time and time again, just like he'd done when she was pregnant with Austin and Jax. But Max left the decision up to Leah and Carly, who was Leah's OB/GYN, and once she hit seven months Leah was given no choice and put on desk duty. That had been the compromise. Matt understood how boring and frustrating working the desk could be, because he'd been put there several times as punishment for things out of his control.

Even so, he didn't like seeing his sister-in-law, who he was close with and cared about as if she was a blood sister, putting herself at risk while pregnant.

Even thinking about it now tightened his jaw and made his fingers clench into fists.

If Leah was his wife, he wouldn't allow it. He would put his foot down and demand her to be assigned desk duty as soon as the pregnancy test showed a plus sign.

Unfortunately, nobody gave a fuck how he felt about it.

He just didn't want to risk any more children. Too many children had suffered or died on his watch. And it was because of that, seeing those children dead or dying that had splintered his brain into a million pieces. It was because of those vulnerable innocents who suffered that made him not want children of his own.

The fear of seeing his own child like that would destroy him.

He was clear with Carly in the beginning that he didn't want any. And she was clear with him that was all she wanted. To be a mother. Even though she was incapable of getting pregnant.

To keep Carly in his life, he had done his best to eventually be okay with having a child of their own.

Or he would've lost her.

And he needed her.

Christ, he needed her.

Without her, he wouldn't have survived returning to civilian life. He would've eaten his gun or been locked in a padded room in a mental hospital.

Without her, he wouldn't have Levi.

So now Levi was his responsibility. His to protect and care for.

And the fuck if he'd let any of those inbred motherfuckers on that mountain steal him or hurt him in any way.

If they even approached the baby, if they even looked in his direction, whether he was five-weeks-old or fifteen, Matt would gather Sig and his brotherhood of bikers and finish what the Blood Fury MC started.

Officer of the law or not, he was now Levi's father first.

"Matt!"

He frowned, wondering why she sounded panicked. Was something wrong with Levi? With her?

His breathing became strained, his vision tunneled.

Oh fuck, he hadn't done this in a really long time...

As he blindly reached for Carly's hand, everything went black.

"Matt... Matt..."

Air in.

Air out.

"Come back to me... Matt, please. Breathe..."

Inhale.

Exhale.

"Just breathe, baby."

He was trying.

He blinked and the darkness began to fade, his vision began to widen.

He knew where he was. He knew who he was with.

He was safe.

Safe.

It had been a long time since he'd had a panic attack. Or

blacked out unexpectedly. The meds usually helped keep him steady.

Levi's arrival had made him wobble, but he'd hidden that from Carly, not wanting to scare her. Not wanting her to rethink their choice of adopting Levi.

He knew how much she wanted a baby and thought he'd been ready. Thought they'd waited long enough. Maybe he'd been wrong.

He was scared.

Of losing her.

Of losing Levi.

Someone else's blood who was now his. It didn't matter that Levi didn't carry a drop of DNA from him or Carly. None of that mattered the second their son was born and Matt caught him, then cut the umbilical cord.

And when Carly held the baby for the first time—still covered in gunk—she cried.

She cried because her dream had been born that day. The dream she held onto for so long. That dream he'd messed up for her. But she hoped...

Hoped he'd get better. One day be ready. Be able to handle it.

Now, he might mess it up again.

"Matt... It's because of Levi, isn't it?"

It wasn't because of Levi. It was the fear of something happening to him.

Christ, he couldn't tell her that and crush her dream. Or make her regret being with him. "I love you," he whispered.

A tear slipped from the corner of her eye as she ran a knuckle down his jaw. "I know."

"I love him, too."

"It's unmistakable."

"I thought I was better." *Damn it*, he thought he had been ready.

She squeezed his hand, the one he had grabbed before he blacked out. His lifeline.

"You are. Things are new. The household has changed. You like things in order, you like schedules. Right now, there's no order and we're just finding our way as a family. We'll get there."

Fuck, he hoped so.

He didn't ever want to hurt her or Levi. He wouldn't be able to live with himself if he did. "I'm worried it might get worse."

She grabbed his chin and turned his face to hers. "It won't." She sounded so confident. "Take your meds, talk to your therapist. Tell him your concerns. You need to be honest with him. For us."

He sucked in a deep breath. "I will."

"That's all I ask. The rest we can work through. Look how far we've come."

She was right. They'd already gone a long way.

But this morning's episode was proof he still had a way to go.

He could only hope he'd get there. And when he did, that Carly and Levi would still be with him to see it.

CHAPTER FOUR

TEDDY & ADAM

Teddy flipped over and pressed his right cheek into his satin-covered, fluffy goose down pillow and stared at Adam sleeping on his "normal," no-frills pillow from Target because he refused to "rest his face on a dead duck."

Since Teddy was the older one of the two, he needed all the restful beauty sleep he could get. Unlike his fiancé, he minded waking up to red creases on his face. But then, the man had slept in tents, or worse, in some horrible desert in the Middle East. And most likely didn't have any kind of skin care regimen out there while fighting the "good fight."

He probably used a bar of generic soap and a hose.

Teddy shuddered.

But now Adam was on a better path of taking care of the only skin he had. It had been a struggle at first, but Teddy managed to convince his lover to at least try a few products to maintain his naturally handsome look.

Not that his lover needed much.

But a good shampoo, conditioner, moisturizer and shaving cream was the very minimum.

And sometimes Teddy would do a sneak attack and schmutz a

little gel into the dark hair Adam kept the same style as his cousins. Trimmed tight on the sides and a bit longer at the top. Which gave away what he did for a living and what he lived for. First serving his country as a Marine, then serving his adopted community as a cop.

Selfless. That was what his man was.

He had secretly lusted after all three of Adam's cousins—who Teddy lovingly called the Bryson bucks—throughout high school. After graduation he finally worked up the courage to "come out" to his parents, after working so hard and so long to hide who he really was, hoping they'd understand, hoping they'd support him, hoping they'd continue to love and accept him.

Unfortunately, he was wrong.

Soul-crushing, self-esteem toppling wrong.

Finding himself homeless and with no family, he escaped Manning Grove and tried to find his way in New York City, where, of course, he'd be accepted, loved and treated like normal. Right? Since NYC was progressive. A melting pot of every type of human under the sun.

He worked his way up from the streets by landing his virgin ass into a hairdresser's bed, who took him under his wing. Teddy learned to do every job in his lover's salon. He even got his cosmetology license.

And then his lover got a new lover, another "lost" virgin, since Teddy was no longer that.

Once again tossed aside, he tried to make ends meet in a city that wasn't kind to those who had nothing. He accepted his failure and eventually went back to the place where he grew up, where he both felt comfortable because it was familiar and uncomfortable because he had no one.

But in a way, it was easier to build a life in Manning Grove, even if it was a life alone. Living close to his family, he hoped one day they'd reach out and try to understand who he was and how he couldn't just change into what they wanted him to be.

He couldn't live that lie.

Which meant he remained alone.

Until one day, he spotted a city girl who appeared lost and overwhelmed in a small town, trying to take responsibility for an adult brother she'd never met. A man who was looked at differently by society, just like Teddy.

Teddy got his claws in that city girl, who let him feel safe enough to be himself and allowed his personality to shine. If he had been straight, he would have married that girl, but he loved her just the same.

Because of her, he suddenly belonged somewhere again.

Somehow they both became a Bryson, swallowed up into that family like they'd been born into it. And he had family once more.

He owed Amanda the world. If it wasn't for her, he might not have met his own soulmate, who slept soundly by his side, looking as delicious in sleep as he had in a well-fitted dark suit across that parking lot at Marc and Leah's wedding.

A Type-A alpha. A cop. A Marine. Not embarrassed to love someone like him, who was, as some have called Teddy, "light in the loafers."

Yes, he was. And he no longer cared who knew.

He was loud and proud.

He didn't care if people hated him for who he was. Or talked behind his back. Or called him nasty names. He didn't care because it was *their* problem.

Not his.

Not Adam's.

And he was going to marry that man.

They were going to live and love the way they wanted and not worry about what others said. Or thought.

Life was too damn short for that.

They could now legally marry and that was what Teddy wanted. Nothing less. He had proposed to Adam and his lover had said yes without even the slightest hesitation.

However, two years later they were still "engaged" and every time Teddy brought up planning their wedding, Adam changed the subject. Or made an excuse of why the time wasn't right or why they couldn't plan it just yet.

Or he would simply say, "Soon."

Teddy didn't want "soon," he wanted "now."

If they were ever going to have kids, they needed to do so soon. At forty-five, he wasn't a spring chicken and finding a surrogate, getting her pregnant through IVF, plus the months of pregnancy, took time. He could be fifty before their first, and probably only, child was born.

He was afraid he'd feel like a grandfather instead of a father.

In truth, Teddy would be okay with never having kids, but Adam hinted that he'd like at least one. And watching his lover around the Bryson babies showed what a great father he'd be.

He sighed and continued to stare at who he hoped would be his future husband.

Adam's dark lashes were thick, his nose perfect, his lips... Well, the man was good with his lips. Extraordinarily good.

Superb.

And Adam never hesitated to reciprocate the *attention* Teddy gave him. Actually, Adam's cock-sucking skills were *two-snaps-and-a-clap* worthy.

Teddy pursed his own lips as he traced Adam's with the tip of his index finger. His fiancé could be intense and take life too seriously sometimes, so when he was sleeping, his body and face were relaxed, making him look ten years younger than he was.

Which would then make Teddy a cougar.

Rawr!

An overnight growth of dark whiskers covered Adam's face. He'd grown it out on occasion, but normally liked his face smooth since it made him look more "squared away" for his position as a police officer.

Yes, Teddy's man wore a uniform. *Purr.* And looked damn good in it, too.

Adam was so damn handsome, looking at him was sometimes like looking directly into the sun. Blinding.

It was more than his rakish smile. Or the Brysons' signature crystal blue eyes. Or that tiny scar that marred his perfectly-shaped eyebrows.

Perfect because Teddy would force his cute butt into a chair and thread those thick bushy eyebrows. Though, Adam made him swear to never tell *anyone* that secret.

Of course, Adam Bryson's eyebrows were naturally shaped that way...

Wink. Wink.

Teddy brushed his knuckles over the dark wiry patch of hair that divided his muscular pecs, the hair that funneled into a line that traveled down the center of his six-pack—yes, his man had a freaking six-pack!—around that cute little half outie/half innie belly button before blooming into the well-groomed patch framing all of his manly goodness.

Teddy loved to imagine he was Little Red Riding Hood following that dark and dangerous path until he came across the largest bear in the woods, who'd jump out, surprise him and gobble him up.

And, yes, he had his fairy tales messed up. He just didn't care. It was his fantasy.

If they ever had a child, that was one fairy tale that would not be told. Not because of violence but because it always turned X-rated.

Sometimes he wondered if his flamboyant personality—his true self—was too much for Adam, who was on the more conservative side. His fiancé saw no need to draw attention to himself and wasn't always comfortable when Teddy tended to be loud and made it known that they, as a gay couple, existed in this town and weren't going to hide.

They were such opposites.

Maybe Adam's delay was because he wasn't sure about their future.

Or maybe Adam was simply with Teddy because he was the only other "out" man in the area. Maybe if there was more of a choice, Adam wouldn't choose him at all.

Yes, they had sexual chemistry, but maybe that was all Adam experienced. Nothing deeper.

Teddy slammed a hand over his mouth so he wouldn't cry out at the pain suddenly stabbing at his heart.

It was easy to say the words, "I love you." It was harder to mean them.

Sometimes those words could be hollow and automatic as to not create conflict.

When Adam said those three words, did he mean them? Or did he say them just to placate Teddy to avoid drama?

Was Adam having second thoughts?

He'd been so secretive lately. Getting home late. Taking phone calls out of Teddy's hearing and not explaining why or who called. Or he would simply brush them off as something to do with work.

But then there were the hours when he just disappeared.

They used to take their lunch breaks together on a regular basis, but recently he'd cancelled a few of them, saying he had an emergency incident he needed to respond to. Only to find out through the Bryson grapevine that Adam hadn't responded to anything at all.

Had the man he loved found someone else? Someone who would fit into his life better? Someone who wouldn't embarrass him, unlike Teddy did with his drama queen theatrics?

Oh God, had he driven Adam into an affair?

If so, Teddy would find the culprit and scratch out the other man's eyes.

But if Adam couldn't love him the way he was, his true self, then he couldn't love Teddy period.

His heart began to race at the thought of losing the man he loved to someone else. Of being alone again.

Of maybe no longer belonging to the Bryson family, the one family who loved him and accepted him as he was.

A whimper bubbled up his throat.

In a panic, he shook Adam's shoulder. "Adam!"

Adam jackknifed up to a seated position, eyes wide but unfocused. "What? What's wrong?"

Teddy also sat up, his fingers digging into his lover's shoulder, his other hand grabbing Adam's prickly jaw and jerking his head in his direction. "Don't you love me anymore?"

Adam's perfectly manicured eyebrows dropped low. "What?"

"You don't love me anymore!" Teddy wailed.

"What?"

"You don't want to marry me! You've found someone else! Who? Who is it? I'm going to scratch his damn eyes out!"

Adam's mouth gaped open and a loud breath escaped before he snapped it shut. "Did you have a bad dream or something?"

"Yes, this is my nightmare."

Adam ran a hand down his face and shook his head. "Well, you're awake now so your nightmare is over. Go back to sleep. It's..." His eyes slid to the digital clock on Teddy's nightstand. "Christ. It's five in the fucking morning." Adam flopped back down, breaking Teddy's hold. He punched his generic-brand pillow back into shape, rolled to his side, giving Teddy his back, settled in and sighed. "Go back to sleep."

"I can't," Teddy cried, gluing himself to Adam's warm, broad back.

"What the fuck, T. I need to work second shift today. I need sleep."

"I can't sleep, lover. I can't."

Adam rolled again until he was facing Teddy with only a few

inches separating them. "I can't deal with your neurosis right now."

"It's not neurosis."

Adam's eyebrows jerked up his forehead.

Teddy grimaced and rolled his eyes. "Okay, okay. I get a little paranoid."

"A little?"

"Well, you've been so secretive lately."

"I have not. I've been busy."

"With what?"

"Work."

Teddy narrowed his eyes at him. "You're lying."

Adam's expression turned hard. "Really? You're calling me a liar?"

Teddy pressed his lips together.

"You know I want to make detective. I've been trying to prove myself to Max."

That was true. Max had mentioned it, too.

Adam continued, "That means odd hours and a crazy schedule sometimes."

That was also true.

But still...

Teddy rolled into him, knocking Adam to his back, and climbing on top to stare directly into those light blue eyes that did all kinds of naughty things to him.

"Do you love me?" He tried to keep the whine out of his voice, but failed.

"Jesus, Teddy. What's up your ass?"

"Not you. It's been *forever* since we've made love."

"It hasn't been *forever*," Adam scoffed.

"*Fore... ev... ver.*" He emphasized each syllable with a finger poke to that hard, muscular chest.

"It hasn't..." His *not-lately* lover went quiet. Adam pursed his beautiful, kissable, suckable lips.

"Gah! You don't want me anymore!" Teddy cried out. "I knew it!"

"Jesus Christ," Adam muttered.

Teddy poked a finger into his fiancé's chest once more, making Adam wince. "Don't invoke him in this bed. He won't help you out of this."

"I don't need help. You're just making more out of this than you need to. I've been... distracted."

"With someone else?"

"Teddy..."

He pressed a finger against Adam's luscious lips. "*Uh uh.* I need you to be honest with me. Do you still love me?"

Adam frowned.

"Do you still want my tight, delectable ass?"

Teddy squealed as Adam hooked him with one of those muscular legs and rolled him until he was pinned to the bed. His fiancé was now settled between Teddy's thighs and had both palms planted in the mattress on either side of his head.

Adam dropped his head until his lips were just a hairsbreadth above Teddy's mouth. He growled, "Do I need to prove it?"

Teddy licked his lips. "That would be swell. And since you're already awake..."

"I ought to spank that irresistible ass for waking me up over imaginary nonsense."

"*Ooh,*" Teddy breathed, his cock waking up at the thought. His man was such a gorilla. A big silverback. Big and strong and... so growly when he was annoyed. "You just got me hard," he announced needlessly. Just in case Adam didn't feel his erection pressing into his lower belly.

Teddy wasn't the only one hard. Adam's long, thick cock was pressed into Teddy's thigh.

"Are you going to make love to me?"

"No."

Disappointment flooded Teddy, making him pout.

"I'm going to fuck you."

"*Oooooh.*" He liked the sound of that better.

"I'm going to take you hard and rough so you'll feel it later today and remember who your ass belongs to when you're watching that parade."

"*Oooooooooooh.*" He *really* liked the sound of that. "I could use a little reminder, lover."

"It won't be a little one."

No, no it wouldn't. No complaint there. "I've missed you," he whispered.

"Baby, we haven't fucked in like three days. Not sure why you're having a meltdown over that."

"You've been distant."

"I just have a lot on my mind."

"Okay, then let's clear it by breaking our long dry spell."

"You must've missed the part where I said I was fucking you."

"I didn't miss it. You're just going *way* too slowly."

"So, my Teddy Bear wants me to rush?"

Oh, he loved when Adam called him his Teddy Bear. "No, not rush, but get the action started."

"The action has already started, T-bear. We're both hard."

"Obvi—" His smart response was smothered by Adam's mouth.

He groaned as their tongues tangled and fought, Adam trying to take control and Teddy giving him some resistance.

He didn't want to be considered easy, after all.

His heart thumped with joy as he grabbed Adam's whisker-covered cheeks and deepened the kiss. Those skillful lips could make a man's toes curl.

Oh, right. They already had!

Adam allowed Teddy to control the kiss for just a smidgeon and then the tables turned.

. . .

Adam forced Teddy's tongue out of his mouth and reminded his fiancé who normally took control.

Normally.

Because on occasion he'd let Teddy top him, but it was extremely rare and usually a special occasion since Adam had to have quite a few beers in him first. Since he was *not* a bottom.

He had learned that early on when he was exploring his sexuality. So for him to bottom for Teddy meant a lot.

But he wasn't bottoming for Teddy this morning. Hell no. Right now he was annoyed that, one, Teddy woke him up for no good reason, and two, Teddy was letting worry about nothing eat at him.

His fiancé tended to get a bit dramatic over the smallest things.

It was one thing he loved about him. And one he also needed a lot of patience about. Because sometimes it could be too much.

Yes, his lover was right. Adam had been very distracted lately and it wasn't due to trying to make detective. It really had nothing to do with that.

But Adam couldn't tell Teddy the truth. Not yet. Tomorrow was Christmas and he didn't want to ruin anything.

Plus, he needed to get through working one more shift before he could start a desperately needed week of vacation. He had a trip planned to Aruba and was keeping that from Teddy. It was part of his surprise Christmas present.

Adam could already hear the high-pitched squeal of excitement. And then picture the worry that would overtake Teddy as he panicked about closing down his shop for a week. But last week he gave Amanda the key to Manes on Main and had her call all of Teddy's appointments to reschedule them without him knowing.

Everything was going as planned. As long as Teddy didn't fuck it up.

Which he could do very easily.

All his future husband had to do is get into one of his "snits" and all the planning Adam had done could get flushed down the toilet.

But now was not the time to worry about any possible Teddy disasters. Right now, he needed to show his Teddy Bear just how much he still loved and wanted him.

Since, apparently, that was in question.

He ended the kiss, ignoring Teddy's noise of complaint, which turned into noises of encouragement as Adam made his way down his lover's long, lean body, scraping his rough morning scruff over Teddy's well-exfoliated and deeply moisturized skin. First planting a kiss on each nipple, then flicking the pebbled tips with his tongue.

Teddy made a purring sound and grabbed the top of Adam's head encouraging him even lower.

He licked the narrow line of hair down the center of his belly and paused, placing a kiss over the scissor tattoo that decorated one hip.

Teddy took his salon business seriously. He was good at it and very successful with plenty of loyal customers who didn't give a flying fuck that their hairdresser was gay.

Even the "blue hairs"—what Teddy called his elderly regulars—thought he was a "hoot." And, luckily, seemed to be very supportive of his and Adam's relationship.

Which made moving to Manning Grove to join the PD a bit easier.

That didn't mean all the area folks accepted them, there were plenty who didn't. Including Teddy's own family who avoided them like the plague. As if homosexuality could be caught like a virus.

For the most part, Teddy's parents avoided town, but the few times they'd run into them, they acted like Teddy was invisible. In fact, one time while he and Teddy were in Dino's Diner on their regular lunch meetup, his parents walked in, spotted the two of them and walked out without a word or even a sign of recognition.

It was heartbreaking and he was glad Ron and Mary Ann had brought Teddy into their family fold. Even Adam's own parents were more than accepting of their relationship and welcomed Teddy as their future son-in-law.

He was lucky his parents weren't judgmental and never had been. So, he couldn't imagine being "shunned" by your own family for being true to yourself.

He would love to have a few words with Teddy's parents but he knew it wasn't worth alienating them any further. Honestly, he just didn't give a shit about them. They would never change their ways or their views, which were narrow.

They might not want Teddy in their life but there were plenty of other people who did.

But now Teddy was feeling insecure about the secrets Adam was keeping. He was keeping those secrets for good reason.

He skimmed his lips from Teddy's tattooed hip to his other one. Fingers pushed at the top of his head. Someone was being impatient.

If anyone should be, it should be Adam. He had to work later and hadn't come home from last night's shift until after midnight. So really, Adam shouldn't be taking his time, they should be having a quickie. But, with the insecurity Teddy was experiencing right now, that might make it worse.

Because of that, he would take his time, settle his fiancé's fears and then go back to sleep so he wasn't dead on his feet tomorrow.

He nuzzled the manscaped hairs at the root of Teddy's erection, took his soft sac into his mouth, heard a hiss come from above, while fingers dug into his scalp, and then he slowly licked up the underside of Teddy's cock, ending at the slick head.

"Lover," Teddy groaned as Adam hovered over the crown.

He tipped his eyes up to the man who was holding his breath in anticipation. He took T into his mouth, sucking him deep, tasting that familiar, salty precum on his tongue. Teddy's hips rose slightly and Adam kept his eyes on him as the man threw his head back on his dead duck pillow and let out a ragged sigh.

He hadn't done this in a while. Now he regretted it. He enjoyed pleasuring his fiancé since he got off on T getting off.

Forgetting to take care of Teddy like this was just proof Teddy was right, Adam had been distracted and not completely "there" in their relationship. Again, he had a good excuse but needed to not be so hyper-focused on not only him working toward becoming a detective, but his secret.

Even right now, he wasn't concentrating one hundred percent on what he was doing. He sighed mentally and forced himself to focus.

He wrapped his fingers around the root and squeezed, then followed Teddy's lead on how fast or slow he wanted.

"That's it, lover," Teddy moaned, his slim hips surging up.

Listening to T's noises as Adam sucked him, made him rock hard and leak against the sheets.

Adam released him with a wet pop.

"What? No!" Teddy complained, his head shooting up off the pillow.

"Prep yourself because I'm going to make you come and as soon as I do, I'm taking what's mine. This is your one and only warning."

"Oh!" Teddy scrambled to dig into his nightstand, grabbing a bottle of lube and, with shaky hands, popped open the cap and squirted a generous amount on his fingers. "Careful. I don't want to knee you in the face."

Adam shifted enough to let Teddy access the area he needed to prep inside and out and, once he was done, he closed the cap and tossed it down near his hip in case Adam would need more. They no longer used condoms since they had both been tested before moving in together, and both agreed to test yearly for peace of mind. But they never went without lube. Though, in a pinch, they'd found some interesting alternatives to commercial lubricants.

As soon as Teddy settled back into place, Adam took him deep into his mouth again and on the upstroke, circled the tip with his tongue. On the down stroke, purposely, but gently, scraped his teeth over T's sensitive head. His whole body jerked and Adam pinned him down to the bed with an arm over T's waist and increased his pace, getting a bit more aggressive with his actions.

That action got the reaction he was hoping for. Which was Teddy losing his mind and forgetting all about his unneeded worry that Adam fell out of love with him or wasn't attracted to him anymore. That was far from the truth.

"Lover..."

Adam smiled around T's cock, which had gotten harder the closer he was to exploding.

"Adam, baby..."

Adam ignored the warnings and continued on his path to bring Teddy to orgasm.

"I..." Teddy whimpered. "Oh... I'm coming..."

That was the whole point, so it wasn't a surprise. Adam didn't let up, didn't slow down, he kept the same pace until Teddy's hips shot up and he cried out Adam's name, who was glad he had short hair, otherwise T might have ripped out a large chunk of it as he came. His future husband's cum coated his tongue and slid down his throat as he accepted all of it.

He didn't even let Teddy come off the rush of his orgasm before Adam was spreading his fiancé's thighs wide and pushing his knees back toward his slender chest, giving Adam the access he needed and wanted.

He moved until he was on his knees, slid his dick down T's lubed crease until he found his target.

"Yes," Teddy hissed. "Please..."

The crown of his cock slipped past the tight ring of muscle and he drove himself into his man, claiming him.

Reminding him of one reason they were together.

They fit. Their differences complemented each other. Even though their personalities were opposite, they somehow worked together.

Teddy kept him from being too serious and he kept T grounded. Only to a point, because he didn't want to stifle Teddy's zest for life. Or who he was.

It was Teddy being in Adam's face and not letting himself be ignored that day at Marc and Leah's wedding that made him consider T as a lover. As a friend. And eventually his partner in life.

Once Adam was deeply seated, he hesitated for only a second, just long enough to interlace his fingers with T's and press their joined hands into the bed. Then he stared into his man's jade-colored eyes. Eyes so expressive, Adam could pick up on Teddy's mood easily just by reading them.

"Hey," he whispered as he moved slowly in and out of T's hot, slick canal, physically connecting the two of them. Now, he wanted to connect them mentally. To show his fiancé he had no reason to worry. Adam wasn't going anywhere.

"Hey, handsome," Teddy whispered back, his eyes getting shinier than they should during sex. This was supposed to be a happy moment, not a sad one.

"You've got no reason to worry."

Teddy bit his bottom lip and nodded his head, but said nothing.

That meant he would still worry.

But then, that was who Teddy was and Adam shouldn't expect any different.

"I love you..."

Another nod of his head, Teddy's green eyes beginning to well.

Jesus, if he started crying...

"I love being inside you."

Again, a nod, this time a tear slipped out, ran down his temple and into his dark blond hair.

Then a sniffle.

And... of course, his face began to twist.

Shit.

"If you start bawling, I'm pulling out and going back to sleep."

Teddy's eyes went wide and he frowned. "Don't you dare."

"Don't you dare cry," Adam ordered.

Teddy pulled one of his hands free and fanned it rapidly over his now damp face. "Well, you're making me emotional!"

"*You* are making yourself emotional."

"How'd I get so lucky to get my very own Bryson buck?"

"You hunted me down, tempted me into a closet, locked the door and then gave me a piece of you. And I'm not talking a piece of your ass. I'm talking," Adam tapped on Teddy's chest over his heart, "this piece of you. Though, your ass was and still is pretty damn sweet, too."

Teddy swiped at his leaking eyes and rubbed at his nose. "It was very romantic, wasn't it?"

"It was hardly romantic but you caught my attention."

"I locked you in a closet and gave you no choice but to pay attention."

"Best day ever," Adam whispered.

Teddy's lip quivered. "Stop saying such sweet things!"

Adam bit back his grin. "Okay."

His eyes widened. "No, don't stop!"

"Make up your mind."

T flapped a hand around again. "Continue."

"How about if we continue what we're doing and talk later?"

"I can get on board with that."

"I wasn't taking a survey."

Teddy's mouth gaped open, snapped shut, then he grinned. "You're such a gorilla."

"But I'm your gorilla."

His grin slipped.

"No more fucking crying," Adam threatened. "Or you're no longer getting the D."

"I want the D," T whispered.

"And I want to give it to you." He dropped a kiss on Teddy's soft lips, then ran his nose along T's before pressing their foreheads together. "I'm going to come inside you."

"You better," T breathed.

Adam caught Teddy's free hand again and once again interlaced their fingers and pinned them to the bed. Then he moved, driving hard and deep into his lover. Loving the tight squeeze of Teddy's ass. Loving the noises he made. Loving how close this special connection made them. Teddy was crazy if he thought Adam was going anywhere.

Just the opposite.

He was already where he belonged.

He thrust quickly until he felt the pressure begin to build, then slowed it down, not wanting it to end. Wanting this to last a little longer. Willing to deal with a little loss of sleep.

They shared a kiss, then another one.

But when Teddy squeezed tightly around him, he was done. He couldn't hang on anymore. He pressed his mouth to his lover's ear and told him, "I'm going to fill you with me."

The man shuddered beneath him at his words, Adam knowing that was what Teddy craved.

With one last surge, Adam drove deep and remained that way, a low grunt escaping his lips, his cock pulsing as he emptied himself inside his fiancé, his future husband, his life partner.

Teddy hadn't been what Adam had been looking for but turned out to be exactly what he needed.

And Adam was never letting him go.

PART TWO

LATER CHRISTMAS EVE

CHAPTER FIVE

MARC & LEAH

Leah groaned as she settled into the folding chair her father-in-law had set up for her in front of Teddy's salon, Manes on Main. She was glad this was her last baby, girl or not.

Ron—always the protector, since it was in his blood—settled into the chair next to her. He handed her a blanket, but she waved it away.

"Give it to Mom, this baby is making me hot." She was actually ready to shuck her wool coat, but if Marc saw that, he'd have a fit.

"She has one already. Sit on it for now. Might help prevent those hemorrhoids."

Leah's mouth opened, then snapped shut. It was best just to ignore that last part.

Ron's sons got their stubbornness honestly.

Marc also got his deep, manly voice from him. And his looks. Ron, now in his mid-sixties, was a hot grandfather. He stayed in shape by keeping busy on their Christmas tree farm.

And by wrangling grandchildren.

Ron folded the blanket, helped Leah stand and then put it on the seat of the chair before helping her sit again. "Speaking of mothers, how's yours?" he asked as he sat back down.

Leah twisted her head and met Ron's blue eyes. "Great. She's loving it down there. She wanted me to remind you that you and Mary Ann need to come visit again soon and spend some time with her on the beach." Her mother had moved to the South Carolina coastline after meeting a man and remarrying.

Leah was happy for her but missed her. And her mother missed seeing her grandchildren on a regular basis. With both Leah and Marc's schedules, it was hard for them to plan a visit or a vacation. When they managed it, it left the PD two officers short.

And now with baby number three coming in the next few months...

"Maybe after the holidays and before my last grandchild is born. Because we're not missing that," he answered.

If it was up to Ron and Mary Ann, they'd be in the delivery room while she gave birth. Having Marc in there with her was more than enough. Sometimes it was too much.

"Are you sure this will be your last grandchild?"

He lifted one thick salt and pepper eyebrow. "Are you having another one?"

"No!" she shouted way too quickly.

Ron grinned. "Didn't think so. Amanda's done. I doubt Carly will push to adopt another baby. Then the only ones left are Teddy and Adam. Any kids they have won't technically be grandchildren."

"Maybe not technically, but close enough."

Ron lifted and dropped one of his broad shoulders. "True. But my brother will be that child's true grandfather."

Leah reached out and patted Ron's hand. "You're everyone's grandfather, Dad. Including Greg."

A wistful smile crossed the older man's face. "That boy..."

"Did you find the tree you were looking for?"

He smirked. "We found something."

Heat crept into Leah's cheeks. "We won't discuss that."

"Good idea. But yes, the kids helped pick the perfect tree."

"Did they get it decorated?"

"We got it set up and the decorations down from the attic, but we'll get them to decorate it after the parade to keep them busy."

"We appreciate you taking them."

"I saw that." Ron winked at her.

"We're not talking about that!"

"Oh, that's right."

The sidewalks were filling up with people, either standing or setting up chairs along the parade route through the center of town.

Ron cleared his throat and, luckily, changed the subject. "At least it stopped snowing."

"I hope it snows tomorrow. Just flurries. It'll make the day even more special if it does."

Leah spotted Mary Ann making her way through the crowd with Greg and Hannah on her heels. The Brysons always staked out the sidewalk in front of the salon every year to watch the parade. It was tradition.

Her mother-in-law stopped in front of her and held out a paper cup. "Hot chocolate."

"A hot toddy would be better."

Marc's mother made a face.

"I'm kidding, Mom." Leah muttered under her breath, "But not really."

"I heard that!" Mary Ann exclaimed as she got Greg settled into his seat with a blanket next to Ron and she took the seat on the other side of Greg. Hannah dropped into the folding chair on the other side of Leah with dramatic flair.

Leah took a sip of the rich hot cocoa and *mmm*'d, then leaned forward to ask Mary Ann, "Where are the boys?"

"They found Marc walking the crowd. They're with him doing foot patrol, pretending they're police officers. He's going to herd them back here shortly."

"I'm sure Oliver doesn't want to miss his father riding in the parade."

"Dad's in it every year," Hannah announced, with two gloved hands wrapped around her own cup. "I'm sure if Liver misses it, he can see it next year."

"I thought you weren't supposed to call him that?" Leah asked the ten-year-old version of Amanda.

"He likes it."

"He doesn't and you aren't," Mary Ann scolded her from a few seats down, sipping on her own hot drink.

"Every time you call him that I'm tossing one of your presents into the fire."

"Grandpa!" Hannah shrieked.

"Too extreme? Okay, then every time you call him that, I'll change the name tag on one of your presents to his name. Then he can have all the awesome gifts we bought for you."

"Grandpa," she moaned. "That's not nice."

"Neither is calling your brother organ meat."

"Eww!"

Suddenly, Leah had a flashback of when she and Marc first worked together when he was always spouting some sort of pig product.

She had started to think he had a form of Tourette's. He later confessed he thought of pork butts, ham hocks, and bacon whenever he needed to distract himself from how much he wanted Leah. He wasn't allowed to have her since he was her supervisor.

Sweet but weird.

Typical Marc.

"Pickled pig's feet," she murmured with a smile.

"What?" Hannah asked, pulling her from her memory.

"Nothing."

"Did they buy me pickled pig's feet for Christmas?" Hannah yelled. "Gross!"

"Gross!" Greg mimicked her and laughed.

"Hannah, we all still have our hearing, we'd like to keep it," Mary Ann reminded her.

"The boys get louder than me."

"There are three of them. One of you."

Hannah rolled her eyes and huffed, "Fine." She turned her eyes back toward the empty street that had been cleared of snow for the parade. "When does this thing start?"

"The same time it does every year," Leah answered her, hiding her amusement behind her cup.

"I wouldn't even come if Dad wasn't in it."

"Yes, you would," Ron told her. "It's a mandatory Bryson family tradition."

"When I'm eighteen I won't have to come out here and freeze."

"Will you still be a Bryson when you're eighteen?"

Her mouth gaped open at her grandfather's question. "Yes."

"Then your ass will be in that seat and you will be here."

"Grandpa!"

"Grampa said ass!" Greg crowed, bouncing in his seat.

Mary Ann sighed. Leah smothered her chuckle by taking a sip of hot chocolate.

Leah turned toward her in-laws. "Thank you for taking the kids, it's been so peaceful."

"P-e-a-c-e or p-i-e-c-e?" Ron spelled out.

"Ron!" Mary Ann scolded him.

"Quiet," Leah corrected her mistake. "Until now."

She spotted her husband squeezing through the crowd, carrying Jax, and keeping a tight grip on Austin's mittened hand who held onto Oliver's.

God, seeing him still made her breath catch. Especially when he was in uniform. And this was why she was pregnant for a third time.

Watching him interact with their sons and nephew would make her eggs shoot out of her ovaries like a machine gun.

"Here they come," Mary Ann said.

"Here they come!" Greg shouted, excited to see the boys, like it had been weeks instead of maybe twenty minutes. "And Marc!"

Oh yes, here he came...

Her husband's gaze locked with hers and he smiled.

She decided right then and there, she was taking a nap after the parade so she could jump his bones as soon as he walked in the door after his shift.

His smile wobbled and he lifted one eyebrow at her, like he could read her mind.

She hoped he could. Because that might keep him warm while he walked the parade beat.

When they got close enough, he put Jax down and let go of Austin's hand so they could run over to her.

"Mommy!" They both tackled her and she guarded her hot chocolate so they wouldn't knock it out of her hand. "We had funnel cake."

"You did? Before dinner?"

Austin, a perfect clone of Marc, nodded. "Daddy got it for us."

"Yes, I see the powdered sugar on your lips." She lifted her gaze to his father. "Daddy knows what sugar does to you. And Daddy also knows your grandparents are getting you Chinese food tonight for dinner."

"Daddy also knows what a little sugar does to Mommy," Marc whispered.

"Is that what you younger generation are calling it now?" Ron asked. "Sugar?" He turned to Mary Ann. "Are we going to have sugar later?"

"I put plenty of sugar in your wet-bottom shoofly pie, honey."

Ron smiled. Marc made a face. And Leah groaned.

"At least that gives me hope," Leah said under her breath.

Ron patted her hand. "Yep. If he's anything like me he won't have any problems in the future."

"Christ," Marc muttered, "Pop, the kids."

"The kids, what? We're talking about sugar and pie. Isn't that what you're talking about, too?"

"Whoa," Leah whispered as she saw a big man with an extremely long beard making his way to an empty spot on the sidewalk. He was holding on to a blonde woman with one hand and a matching little girl with the other.

Marc turned his head in the direction Leah was staring to see the six-foot-three, two-hundred-something pound biker heading toward an empty spot not far from where his family sat.

"Dunn and I ran into him the other week in the empty lot where the old warehouse used to be," Leah said.

"What was he doing there? The Blood Fury hasn't owned that lot for a while now."

"He was talking to that blonde. He said she had gotten lost and was only trying to help her. I didn't think they knew each other, but apparently my instinct was wrong."

Marc's eyebrows rose. The PD dealt with Judge Scott and his cousin, Deacon, a lot since they owned Justice Bail Bonds on the other side of town. However, they both began to wear the Blood Fury MC's colors last year when the MC was resurrected by the deceased former president's son. Not one cop at Manning Grove PD was thrilled to hear or see that club be reborn since the Fury had caused a lot of problems prior to it imploding over twenty years ago.

Murder and mayhem had been their M.O.

"She doesn't look so lost right now since she's holding Judge's hand. The little girl must be hers. She looks just like her."

"First time I saw the girl," his wife answered.

As Judge began to set up their folding chairs, the little girl spotted them and took off at a run, little bells jingling on her sneakers.

Both Judge and the mother screamed, "Daisy!" at the same time.

Daisy ran up to both of Marc's sons and Oliver and yelled, "Hi!" at the top of her lungs and did a floppy side wave. "I'm Daisy!"

Austin and Jax both glanced up at Marc, unsure what to do.

Marc shook his head. At this rate, his sons would need help learning how to flirt with girls. He nudged his oldest. "Say hi back."

Before any of the boys could say anything, Daisy announced, "I'm five. Will you be my friends? I don't have any friends to play with yet."

Leah shot Marc a look.

He took the reins since his sons apparently lost their tongues. He placed a hand on Austin's shoulder just as Judge and the blonde reached them. "This is Austin. He's six." He put his other hand on Jax's knit-cap covered head. "This is Jax. He's four. That's Oliver, he's the same age as you."

"Hi!" Greg bellowed, getting to his feet and coming to stand near Marc, shifting his weight from foot to foot. "I'm Greg! I'll... I'll be your friend."

Daisy dropped her head back and stared up at Greg. "Hi, Greg! How old are you?"

"I'm..." Greg tilted his head, and wrung his hands together as he tried to remember. "I'm..."

"Thirty-two," Marc whispered to him.

"Thirty-two!" Greg echoed.

"Oh! You're old!" Daisy said and stuck out her bottom lip in a dramatic pout.

"Daisy!" her mother scolded her.

"Well, he is, Momma!"

Greg laughed. "I'm old."

"Hi, Greg," the blonde greeted. "I'm Cassie. And Daisy is my daughter."

"Hi, Cassie!" Greg greeted with a half-wave and a big smile. "You're really pretty. You here to watch Max in the parade?"

"Thank you. I'm not sure who Max is?" Cassie asked, her brow lowered.

"Max is the Chief of Police around here," Judge explained. His green eyes hit Marc's and he jerked his chin up in greeting. "Marc."

"Judge. Surprised to see you here."

"Ain't my thing, but Dutch is playin' S—" He snapped his mouth shut and glanced at the kids. "Daisy wanted to sit on Santa's lap, give him a list of demands, and also watch the parade."

Marc nodded, glad the biker didn't blow the secret that Dutch, the local garage owner, was playing Santa like he did every year, and that Santa wasn't real. The kids didn't know yet and he wasn't sure if even Greg knew the truth.

Marc glanced down at Daisy who looked tiny standing in front of Judge, then up at Cassie. "New in town?"

"My sister and her husband live here. Daisy and I came right after Thanksgiving."

"Staying?" Marc asked.

"I don't know yet."

Marc didn't miss the look Judge gave her with that answer.

Leah spoke up. "I saw you that night in the empty lot. I was the pregnant one in uniform."

Cassie turned to her. "Yes. The night I got... uh... lost."

"Mmm hmm," Leah answered. "Lost. You show her how to get around town, Judge?"

Judge's lips twitched. "Yeah. She's learnin' her way."

"How are things with the MC?" Marc asked. "Staying off that mountain?"

"Yeah, no more repos up there," Judge said, his face unreadable and not because of the long, bushy beard covering it or the gray knit cap pulled low over his forehead. "Trip learned his lesson."

That wasn't what Marc meant, but he had made his unspoken

point that he knew what happened last month up there between the Shirley Clan and the MC. He didn't know all the details but he knew something went down.

But if it wasn't for the MC, or the Shirleys, Levi wouldn't have come into Matt and Carly's life, so he wasn't going to give Judge a lot of shit about it. Or even dig.

No one had come down that mountain to file a police report and he doubted they would. The Shirleys lived by their own law and hated the PD.

Just like the MC did.

However, Marc was grateful for Autumn letting his youngest brother adopt her baby. They all were.

"Carly's bringing Levi," Marc warned. "Autumn and Sig coming to watch the parade?"

"Don't think so. Don't think Sig wants her in town right now. See you're workin' the parade. Guess your brothers are, too. Figurin' you don't need me to watch over Levi. But if you do, I'm here, just in case."

Marc studied the man for a long moment. Judge had taken on the role of Sergeant at Arms for the MC. That meant he was the muscle behind the club and was in charge of protecting its members and everyone else who fell under that umbrella. Marc had done some research on motorcycle clubs after Trip came back to town and began to rebuild the Fury. He wanted to be prepared. They all did.

He knew the women and children who belonged to club members were considered "property" of the club. And by Judge offering to keep an eye on Levi, the man probably still felt responsible for protecting Marc's newest nephew, even though the baby was now a Bryson.

Protected by a family of cops instead of bikers.

"My wife will be here with them. As will my Pop. He might be retired but he's still a cop and a Marine at heart. So, I think we got it covered. Adam and Matt will be sticking close, too."

Judge pulled at his long beard and nodded. "Got it handled, then."

"Yeah, but appreciate the offer."

Judge tipped his head and stretched a hand out to Daisy. "C'mon, kid."

The little girl pursed her lips. "I want them to be my friends."

"'Nother time," Judge told her. "Sure you'll hang with them when you start school."

That had Marc's ears perking and he noticed Leah's had, too. "So, she is staying in the area?"

"Yeah, she's staying," he answered, putting his arm around Cassie's shoulder.

The woman hadn't said a word to that, so he wondered if she was aware that the big man was making the decision for her.

"Well, it was nice meeting you, Cassie." He offered her his hand and she shook it. "Marc Bryson. That's my wife, Leah, who you've met. My parents, Ron and Mary Ann. Hannah, my niece, and you've met Greg, Hannah's uncle. Welcome to Manning Grove. Great town. Great people." He lifted his gaze to Judge. "We'd like to keep it that way."

Judge's jaw shifted but he gave Marc a sharp nod. "Same here." Then he picked Daisy up, wrapped a large hand around the back of Cassie's neck and took them back to where he had set up their chairs a few yards down the block.

Marc glanced at his wife.

She murmured, "Interesting."

"Having women and children might keep the club on the straight and narrow," Marc hoped.

"Didn't last time," Ron said. "Judge was one of those kids. Trip, Cage, Rook and Sig, too. I'm going to tell your brother to keep a close watch on that MC. Let's hope history doesn't repeat itself. Never thought I'd see the day when our town would be dealing with not only an MC but that crazy clan on the mountain. Once the Fury disintegrated, we thought the worst thing the force would have to deal with was moonshiners and meth makers."

"Yeah, those were the good ol' days, right, Pop?"

Ron shook his head. "Max has got his work cut out for him."

"Let's just hope Dutch was being honest when he told you that they weren't going to bring trouble into town."

"We'll see," his old man said. Oliver climbed into Ron's lap, while Jax was already settled on Mary Ann's.

"Going to go walk, see if I can spot the beginning of the parade. They should start moving through any time now."

"Carly, Amanda and Teddy aren't here yet," Mary Ann exclaimed. "They better hurry or they might miss Max."

Marc scanned the crowd. "Carly's coming. She just stopped with Judge. Looks like she's showing him the baby."

"Well, Teddy needs to open the salon so she can take Levi in where it's warm. I don't want him outside in this weather."

"It'll toughen him up, woman," Ron told his wife.

"A five-week-old baby does not need to be toughened up," Mary Ann scoffed.

"Bah!"

"No pie for you later," Marc's mother said.

"I want pie, I'm eating pie," his father answered.

Marc clapped his hands together. "Okay, then. I'm heading down the street. You all have fun." He leaned over to give Leah a kiss and when he did, he whispered, "Things go sideways, text me. Don't jump into anything."

"What's going sideways? Your parents fighting over *pie*?" Leah had air-quoted the last.

Marc pressed a kiss to her lips. When he straightened, he said, "Just text me if you need me."

"How about if I just tell you I need you?" she whispered with a smile. "If I'm asleep when you get home, wake me."

That sounded promising.

"Don't eat too much sugar before bedtime," his father butted in. "Might not get any sleep. And we got a big day tomorrow."

Leah's lips twisted.

"Yeah, it's Chriss-mas!" Greg shouted. "Santa's comin'!"

"Yeah, Santa's coming!" Jax yelled.

"Down the chimney, right, Grandpa?" Austin asked.

"Only if you've been good this year," Ron said.

"I'll check back later. Be good for your grandparents, boys."

With a last look at his family, Marc shook his head and headed back in the direction he came. The opposite direction from a whirlwind named Teddy, who was heading their way.

CHAPTER SIX

MATT & CARLY

Carly carefully steered the stroller through the crowd, trying to avoid everyone's toes and shins. This was the first time she'd actually used the hand-me down from Amanda and Max.

She felt like a Nervous Nellie taking her baby out in public for the first time. She wished Matt could be there with her, but the reality was he needed to work today to have tomorrow off.

And tomorrow would be a special day none of them should miss.

She hoped she hadn't forgotten to pack everything she needed in the diaper bag and also hoped Levi was warm enough. But as long as Teddy opened the salon, they'd be out of the late December weather soon enough.

A tall man with an extremely long beard caught her attention first, then she recognized the vest he wore. He was standing next to a curvy blonde and a just-as-blonde little girl.

She had seen him and his cousin around town so she knew who he was, she just didn't realize he had joined the local MC that Sig and Autumn, Levi's birth mother, were a part of.

Her first instinct was to keep moving past them, but her curiosity had her pause. "Hi."

The big man wearing a beanie turned his head and ran his gaze over her, then it landed on Levi in the stroller.

"You're Judge, right? You own Justice Bail Bonds?"

"Yeah," Judge grunted and turned to face her.

"I... uh... I'm Carly Bryson." She waved her hand toward the stroller. "This is Levi."

Judge's nostrils flared and his eyes dropped again to the baby.

"Hi! I'm Daisy!" the little girl called out from her chair with a sloppy wave as she kicked her little legs back and forth.

"Hi, Daisy."

What she assumed was the little girl's mother introduced herself. "I'm Cassie."

"Hi." She jutted out her hand to the seated woman. "I'm Dr. Carly Bryson. A local OB/GYN. I'm Autumn's doctor. Stella's, too."

"I'll keep that in mind."

Carly laughed. "I wasn't trying to get you into my stirrups. I just wanted to point out how I know the ladies of your club."

Cassie jerked her chin toward Judge, who now squatted in front of the stroller, staring at the baby. "His club."

"Oh, well. Right. His club. Will Autumn be coming today? I haven't seen her in a while."

"No," came the deep grunt.

"Oh, well..."

Judge reached out and ran a finger down Levi's pudgy cheek. "He got red hair?"

"No."

"Good." Judge nodded, his hand pressed to Levi's chest. It was big enough to cover the whole thing. "He good?"

"Yes, he's very good. Perfect."

Judge nodded again.

"Is Autumn doing okay? I haven't talked to her in a couple weeks. Sig did the last couple drop-offs of her breast milk. I just wanted to make sure everything with her... between them... was okay."

"She's good."

"Can you let her know she's invited over to the Bryson farm tomorrow for Christmas? That's if she wants to spend some time with Levi."

Judge rose to his feet. "Sig ain't lettin' her go anywhere without him."

"Right." And there was no way Sig, an ex-convict, was going to spend Christmas day surrounded by cops. "Well, please still tell her she's welcome, even if she can't come. I just want her to know... How thankful we are."

"She knows." Judge was still staring down at Levi with a relieved expression. Maybe he'd been worried that Levi was going to be born with birth defects. Which had been a valid concern. "You take care of him."

"I plan on it."

"Those inbreds on that mountain give you any shit, you let me know."

Carly's mouth opened and she let it hang there for a second not sure how to respond to that. She belonged to a family of cops. If the Shirleys gave her or Levi any trouble, the last person she'd go to was a biker. She didn't want any more violence than there had already been. Levi was a result of it. More violence was not the answer.

"Okay, well..."

"*Hellllooooooo* there, handsome. Oh!" Teddy stared open mouthed at Judge. "*Ooooh.*" He wrinkled up his nose. "Oh no. No, no, no!" He circled his hand in front of Judge's face. "This mess is not acceptable."

Did Teddy even realize who he was dealing with? Judge was not one of his elderly regulars he did a style and set on. The biker was far from being one of the man's "blue hairs."

"Who told you that looks good? Hmm? You know who?"

Teddy got right into Judge's face and poked him dead center in the chest. "Nobody!"

Judge blinked at him, his face a stiff mask.

Cassie had a hand slapped over her face and was turning a light shade of purple, but had given Teddy a slight nod. Apparently, she agreed.

Daisy sat quiet in her chair with her mouth hanging open, entranced by the wonder of all wonders named Teddy.

"You're hiding that handsome face of yours. Those green eyes, those cheekbones. Those luscious lips." He curved a hand around one side of his mouth and leaned toward Cassie. "Bet he knows how to use them, too."

Cassie nodded again, her hand still covering her mouth.

"Lucky, lucky girl, you. But, handsome, this... *stuff* on your face. Just no. It needs to go."

"I like to pet it," Daisy volunteered. "It's scratchy, though. Nothing like Jury's hair."

Carly had no idea who Jury was.

"Yes, because that's what it looks like, some animal growing on his face."

As Teddy reached up to touch Judge's beard, the bigger man stepped back. "Don't."

"Hmm. Playing hard to get... My favorite type of gorilla. But don't worry, the only pair of scissors I have on me right now is tattooed onto my hip and only one man gets to see those." Teddy turned to Cassie. "What does his hair look like under that knit hat?"

"It's buzzed like he took a dog clipper to it."

Teddy gasped and slapped a hand to his forehead. "You need some serious help, big man. And I'm just the fella to help you." He pointed to the salon not even a half block away. "You see that place there? Manes on Main?"

"Teddy, lived here all my f— *freaking* life. Know who you are, know where your place is."

Teddy's dark eyebrows pinned together. "You have?"

"Yeah. Probably don't know that 'cause I never stepped a foot into your shop." Judge leaned closer and growled, "And never plan to. Got my shit covered. Don't need your help."

Teddy's mouth made a big *O*, then he plugged a hand on his hip. He must have realized he'd get nowhere with Judge, so he turned to Cassie. "You like that stuff on his face?"

Cassie pinned her lips together.

"See? *She* doesn't even like it."

"I like it!" Daisy exclaimed.

"I like it," Judge grumbled. "And it ain't goin' nowhere."

Teddy huffed out a breath. "Well!" He dug out his wallet and pulled out a business card, shoving it at Cassie, who took it. "I'm here for you if you need me. You must be new around here, since I've never seen you or your daughter before."

"I am."

"Then I'm your fella to take care of all that luscious hair for you and your girl. First cut is on the house. Manes on Main." He pointed down to his shop. "Right there." He clapped his hands together once. "Now, I need to go open my salon so this little muffin can get out of the cold." Teddy turned back to Judge. "How long have you lived in town?"

"My whole life," the big man answered.

Teddy pursed his lips and let his gaze rake over Judge again. He tilted his head. "We go to school together?"

"You're a few years older than me."

"Bet I'd recognize your handsome face if you let me trim off that mess."

"Sounds like a good reason to keep it."

Teddy gasped dramatically. "Oh, that's how it is. I see. Fine. Well, then, I'm off." He turned to Carly. "I'm going to go unlock the door for you. See you down there."

He made a little squeak, turned as if he was flipping a cape back behind him and flounced down the sidewalk.

Carly unpinned her lips and said, "Please pass on my invitation to Autumn. Have a Merry Christmas."

"Same to you," Cassie said.

Carly continued pushing the stroller down the sidewalk, which was now even more crowded. When she got to the salon she found her family staked out, wrapped in blankets, and with red-tipped noses.

Matt was right. The weather was too cold for Levi to spend any amount of time outside. However, tomorrow they'd have no choice. She'd bundle up Levi and then strap him to Matt's chest to keep the baby warm.

"Have you seen Amanda?" Mary Ann asked her.

Carly waved a hand back over her shoulder. "I think she was having a little pow-wow with Adam back there on the corner. They had to get a few more details straight."

"How many more details are there?" Ron grumbled. "It's a—" He shut up as Teddy came rushing out of the salon.

"I turned the heat up for you and the little one. Let me know if it gets too warm."

"Thanks, Teddy."

"Well, you take such good care of my broody Bryson buck, so I should be thanking you."

"If you want to sit outside with the rest of the family, I can take Levi inside," Mary Ann offered.

"No. You enjoy your time out here."

"My old bones don't like the cold much anymore."

"Time to go south, Mom," Carly told Mary Ann.

"No! I have my whole family together, I'm not breaking it apart. And I would never miss the opportunity to be around the grandchildren." Mary Ann leaned forward. "No offense, Leah. I don't think your mother was happy up here. She wasn't used to our small town ways."

Leah put a hand on her belly. "She'll head up when this one's close to being born. I don't think she wants to miss that, either."

She gave Carly a look and raised her eyebrows. "Only one person's allowed in the room at the birthing center, right?"

"Uh..." Carly knew not only Ron and Mary Ann, but Leah's mother would want to be there when baby number three was born. They tried getting in the last two times, but Leah had put her foot down. "Just the father."

"There were more than that in the room when Levi was born," Mary Ann complained.

"Those were special circumstances," Carly said quickly. "And I was the doctor."

"Honey, I'm sure Leah doesn't want her in-laws to see her like that. Kind of like this morning." Ron grinned.

Carly knew that grin. She glanced over at her sister-in-law. "What happened this morning?"

"Nothing we're talking about," Leah muttered and shot Carly a look.

"Oh..." Yes, Carly was now used to having so much family, there was always risk of getting caught in a compromising situation if they weren't careful.

In fact, Ron had found her panties hanging from a ceiling fan one morning when he let himself into the house after she and Matt had sex. Carly had no idea how they got up there. They quickly learned to lock doors and pull blinds any time they got naked because they never knew who was just going to show up unannounced.

"I'm taking him inside."

Teddy rushed over to hold the door open for her. "I started the coffee if you want any." He followed her in and immediately began to unbuckle Levi. "Oh, I just want to pinch those chubby cheeks."

Teddy removed Levi from the stroller, planted a loud kiss on one of those chubby cheeks, and held him as Carly peeled the baby out of his snowsuit and down to his onesie. He then carried Levi around the salon, giving him a tour. "I'm going to be the first one to cut those dark locks of yours. And if you ever want to be a hairdresser, Uncle Teddy will be glad to show you the ropes."

"I'm sure Matt has other plans for him."

"Let me guess. Joining the Marines and becoming a cop." Teddy did an exaggerated yawn. "Same old song and dance."

"It's in the blood," Carly reminded him.

"Yes, but this one's blood's a little different, so he needs to be an original. He needs to be the Bryson buck who broke rank."

"I just want him to be healthy and happy."

"Exactly what I wanted for Matty, too." Teddy brought Levi back to her and she took her son from him. "And I was serious when I said I should be thanking you. You have made him as healthy and happy as he can be. I think you saved his life."

Teddy wasn't normally this serious, so hearing him subdued like that made Carly's eyes burn and her nose sting. "Teddy," she whispered.

"Well, it's true. You became the most important member of this family. We might have lost him if it wasn't for you taking him by the nuts and giving his life focus."

Unfortunately, Teddy wasn't the first to say that. "I worry about how the baby will affect his mental health. Even though he won't admit it, sometimes hearing Levi cry takes him back there. I've seen his face and he does his best to fight it, but..." Her husband would always struggle with his PTSD and babies were one of his triggers. Seeing children devastated by war had scarred him deeply.

Teddy's smile was sad as he stared at Levi in her arms. "He loves you. He loves his son."

"Sometimes love isn't enough."

Teddy gave her a squeeze, careful of the baby. "It will be in this case."

Carly hoped he was right.

"Now, today is supposed to be a happy day, so let's stop being so morose. Matty will pull through for his family. He always does." He got on his toes and planted a noisy kiss on Carly's cheek. When he pulled back, his green eyes went wide. "Oh! I think I hear the marching band. I'll be right outside, watching for the eldest Bryson buck in his spiffy dress uniform. If you need anything, just *hollaaa*."

Then the hairdresser was gone, the jingle of the bell above the door the only thing left in his wake.

Carly looked down into Levi's face. The baby was awake and quiet, just absorbing the new atmosphere while contently sucking on his fist. "Let me grab your binky, my sweet baby boy."

She pulled the diaper bag from the stroller and put it on the table sitting in front of the salon's large picture window that had Manes on Main hand-painted in decorative script across the glass. Even decorated for Christmas with colorful lights and snowflake window clings, she'd get a clear view of the parade.

Hannah saw the movement through the window and waved at her. Carly returned it with a smile.

She would love to have a girl, too. This family needed more girls, but she wouldn't push Matt into a second adoption. They were both getting older and she was just relieved and happy when he announced last year that he was ready to go ahead with adopting.

And now her dream had come to fruition.

Digging around in the bag, her fingers brushed against a piece of paper, so she grabbed it along with the binky. Once the pacifier was plugged securely between Levi's little lips and he was sucking quietly, she unfolded the notepaper she had not placed in the bag this morning.

She recognized the scratchy handwriting immediately and her heart stopped. She held her breath as she skimmed the note, then started back at the top to read it more slowly. Once again, tears threatened to spill, making the words difficult to read.

To my love, my life, my wife, the mother of my son,

I could never say in words just how much you mean to me and how much you are a part of me. How much you push me to be a better man. But I want you to know, you do.

I cannot love you any more than I do already.

Thank you for helping me hang on, and for you hanging on along with me through the rough spots.

I'll love you forever.

Your Marine, your husband, the father of your son.

~ M

"Holy shit," Carly whispered, wiping away the tears that finally escaped. That note was the best Christmas present she ever received. She was saving and cherishing it forever. She might even sleep with it under her pillow.

The bell jingled again and she quickly swiped at the rest of the tears and blinked away the blurriness, only to see her brave Marine, her beautiful husband and the loving father of her son walk through the door.

He *was* the love of her life. Faults and all.

Levi wiggled in Carly's arms and Matt noticed his son's eyes fastened on him once he got closer. But while he was happy his son was beginning to recognize him, Carly's tears caught his attention and his spine became a steel rod.

"What's the matter? Are you alright? Is he alright? What happened?"

Carly sniffled and smiled. "We're perfect, you asshole. This was supposed to be a happy day and you made me cry."

He grinned. "Guess you found my note."

"Matt..."

"I meant every word."

Carly blew out a breath and wiped at her eyes. "I know."

"That shouldn't make you cry."

"Of course, it should! I know you don't take saying things like that lightly. That's what made it worse. Or better. Or... whatever. It was perfect."

He stared at her red-rimmed blue eyes and her quivering bottom lip that he wanted to taste. So, he did, leaning in to give her a quick kiss.

When Levi made a happy squeak between them, Matt took him from her arms and held him to his chest, turning toward the large window. "Hey, Levi. You won't remember this parade, but it's the first of many. Uncle Max will be up front."

Carly moved to stand next to him and he put his arm around her shoulders, giving her a squeeze.

"I can't stay long but I wanted to check in on you two." He turned to her. "Sorry about this morning. I promise I'll let the doctor know what happened."

He'd keep that promise, too. He didn't want to fuck up what he and Carly had. She took on a lot when she took on him. And just like he said in the note, he was grateful as fuck that she hung on through his rough times. Every single one.

She ran her fingers over Levi's dark downy hair, tears still in her eyes. "Thank you for doing everything you've done to work on getting better. For doing everything in your power to make it so we could bring a child into our life."

Matt hoped that his son's eyes stayed blue like Autumn's, so they'd be like his. "I know how much it meant to you. I needed to do it for you. I didn't want you to regret never having the child you so desperately wanted. Regret giving up that dream because you married a broken man. I've only wanted you to be happy."

"Same here," she whispered, turning toward him and cupping his cheek. "I love you, Matt. And I would have given up that dream to keep you."

Now there was a damn sting in his eyes. Must be the forced hot air from the salon's heating system. "Knowing you would've made that sacrifice for me was what made me work harder. I didn't want you to do that. I think it would've eventually killed me knowing I destroyed your dream of being a mother."

"I just feel we owe Autumn so much. I extended the invite to her for tomorrow, but I doubt she'll come."

"That shouldn't be surprising. Plus, I think Sig's worried about her leaving the farm right now. Things are still very fresh for everyone involved."

"Thank goodness everything turned out okay. Let's hope it stays that way."

He ran a knuckle down his wife's damp cheek. "It will. This kid's a Bryson. He's got an army behind him."

Carly laughed. "That's true. When I ran into Judge outside, he said he'd step in at any time."

Matt didn't need an MC stepping in to take care of his family. He understood why Judge would offer, but it was unneeded.

"I need to go." He might go have a word with the club's Sergeant at Arms. Just a little reminder that Matt had his family covered.

She wiped at her face. "Can you give me a minute to run to the restroom?"

"Yeah."

As Carly rushed toward the back of the salon, the bell jingled above the door and his mother walked in.

"There's my baby boy with his baby boy," she cried, her face all lit up.

"Ma, there's only one baby in this place. It's Levi."

His mother came over and pinched his cheek anyway, making him pull back. "You'll always be my baby."

"There are plenty of grandchildren you can smother... I mean *baby*."

Mary Ann whacked his arm lightly. "I'll never stop smothering my sons."

Matt groaned.

"I'm so happy that your life is coming together, Matt. That you created your own family. You *are* my baby... But, truthfully," she took a shaky breath, "you scared me for the longest time."

"I know." *For fuck's sake*, now he'd upset the two most important women in his life. He seemed to be an expert at it. It was not a skill he was proud of.

Every time he reenlisted his mother took it hard. No, not just hard, it devastated her. She couldn't understand why he did it, but Matt hadn't been ready to deal with civilian life. He had joined the Marines and became a Raider for a reason, and he struggled with leaving an incomplete job behind. But now, after years of therapy, he realized that job would never be done. There'd always be another conflict, then the next. He couldn't fix things over there and he needed to stop letting that burden, that pressure, eat at him.

"I'm not scared anymore."

Thank fuck for that. "I'm sorry I worried you." He closed his eyes and just breathed for a moment. He'd avoided this conversation for a long time. Too long. But now he had a son, he better understood the love between a parent and a child.

He couldn't avoid it anymore and he owed his mother that much. "I know you think I chose serving over there over you. Over our family. I know that hurt you. I'm sorry I did that to you. It wasn't my intention. My intention was to do my service like every other Bryson and follow in Pop's and Granddad's footsteps. It was what was expected. But when I came home, when I went through the police academy, I felt like it was fake. It wasn't real. War was real. People dying was real. Driving around a quiet town, going to calls of cats caught in a tree weren't. It all felt meaningless, and those incidents were just unimportant. I felt that what I had done over there was more important. It was real." He had a hard time explaining how he felt, like his life in Manning Grove wasn't important, anyone else could step in and do it, but his life overseas gave him meaning.

His heart knew it was wrong, but his brain said otherwise.

"It broke you. And that broke my heart." Her eyes were brimming.

He didn't want to see his mother cry. *Fuck.* "I'm sorry."

A noise had Matt turning his head. Carly stood at the back of the salon, crying, a hand covering her mouth. She dropped it as she came forward and said, "This is supposed to be a happy day!"

His mother squeezed his arm, then got up on her toes and kissed his cheek. "Thank you," she whispered. "I'm sorry if I ever pressured you boys to get married and give me grandchildren. I thought that was why you stayed away. I should've known you three would settle down once you met the perfect partners. And you did. I couldn't be happier with the women you've chosen. And now?" She glanced at Levi in his arms with a soft smile. "I have what I've always hoped for."

"And you still have Pop."

Mary Ann laughed past her tears. "Yes, I still have him." She turned to Carly. "If you need me, yell."

"I will."

"I'm going to walk Ma out." He planted a kiss on Levi's forehead and placed him back into the stroller. He pressed a kiss to Carly's lips and whispered, "I'll see you later."

With a last look at his family, he walked his mother out the door.

CHAPTER SEVEN

TEDDY & ADAM

Teddy couldn't control his foot tapping nervously on the sidewalk. But it was better than chewing his nails down to the quick. Plus, if he did that, all he would do is get a mouthful of *blech* since he was wearing leather gloves.

He wanted to feel better after his conversation—and hot sex— with Adam early this morning, but something still niggled at him. He needed to talk to his best girlfriend.

Where the hell was Amanda, anyway?

She tended to be late, but not this late. And he could see and hear the high school marching band now coming up the street.

The parade order was always the band with the "Happy Holidays" banner and all the high schoolers in their cute uniforms freezing their asses off, then the mayor on a float with the town council. Not freezing their asses off since they got to dress for the weather and probably took nips from their whiskey-filled flasks they had secretly stashed in their coat pockets. Unlike the teenagers.

After them, came Max, the town's Chief of Police, usually freezing his sexy tush off as he sat on the back of a convertible, handing out Manning Grove PD patches to anyone who came up to the car and asked for one. If it was a kid, the child got a little bag of candy, too. Max tended to be very popular with the under eighteen crowd and also with women over eighteen. But for two different reasons.

One for handing out candy, the other for looking like eye candy.

Amanda had gotten herself a catch. But there was no way she was retracting her claws from her man. Not that Max ever looked at other women the same way he looked at his wife.

Teddy sighed.

He wanted what they had. He thought he would get it with Adam. He was starting to wonder.

Ugh, he overthought *everything*! If he wasn't careful, he could push his lover away.

Oh, thank the best friend gods, there Amanda was, fighting her way through the crowd, her eyes on him and wearing a secretive smile.

What. The. Hell?

"You better explain that and you better do it right now!" he insisted as she settled into the seat next to him.

"Should I say hello to my spawn first?"

"No!"

Amanda laughed. "So, what do I need to explain?"

Teddy circled his hand in front of her face. "That look you're wearing, like you know a good secret. You need to share that with your BFF."

"Okay, I will..." Amanda leaned forward and called out to Leah. "Hey, Leah!"

A loud gasp escaped Teddy.

"Hey, Amanda!" Leah called back, unaware of the drama unfolding at their end of the group.

"Baby good?" Amanda asked. She shot a wicked look at Teddy.

Leah gave her a thumb's up. "She's good. I don't know about me."

"That wasn't funny," Teddy hissed. "BFF means best friends *forever*. That means it's *for-ev-er*. You are stuck with me."

"Damn," Amanda muttered.

"Okay, dish, girl. What was with the secretive smile?"

Amanda leaned back in her folding chair, unfolding the blanket that had been left on it and throwing it over her legs. "Nothing. I was just thinking about the surprise we're giving *you-know-who* tomorrow."

You-know-who was Greg. Teddy chewed on that for a second. "I'm not sure that was it."

Amanda sighed. "I swear. That was it."

"Swear on your children's life."

"I'll swear on Hannah's but not Oliver's."

"Mom!" Hannah screeched next to Teddy. "I'm telling Dad!"

"See? This is why. You're a snitch," she told her daughter, struggling to keep a straight face.

"Snitches get stitches," Ron announced from the other side of Leah.

"Grandpa!"

Ron shrugged. "Well, it's true."

Leah, who was sitting between them, had her head dropped forward and she was shaking.

"It's not funny, Aunt Leah," Hannah huffed.

"I disagree," Leah said on an escaped laugh.

Hannah crossed her arms over her chest and pouted.

"Santa sees you pouting," Ron reminded her.

Hannah quickly smoothed out the pout and then glared straight ahead, instead.

"I have no idea where she gets that from," Amanda said under her breath.

Teddy snorted.

The marching band passed them, and they weren't able to talk for a few minutes as the band was loud and they'd pause on every block for the girls to swing batons and flags and whatever else girls did in a marching band while wearing skimpy outfits.

He'd look good in one of those outfits.

Hmm.

Once the band moved on, the mayor's float went by.

Next up was the 1965 Chevy Impala SS Convertible—Teddy hated that he knew those details, but it was the same vehicle the chief always rode in—with Dutch's son driving. Dutch always volunteered Cage and his classic car for the parade every year. The only difference this year—and last—was that Cage had joined the MC that Dutch used to belong to.

He was now one of those leather-clad gorillas. As was the rest of Dutch's manly, *good-with-their-hands* mechanics.

However, Cage was not wearing his club "colors" today out of respect for Max. Dutch did his best to stay on good terms with the PD since he worked on their vehicles, both police and personal.

But Cage was sexy as all get out, as was the rest of Dutch's crew. Sometimes Teddy had the urge to flatten one of his own tires just to get one of them out to "rescue" him. Or at least bend over as they changed his tire.

However, Adam was proficient with changing flats, so if he found out Teddy called someone other than him, he might be a bit miffed.

"There's Uncle Max!" Austin yelled.

"Max!" Greg echoed him, bouncing in his seat and waving at every participant in the parade.

"Hi, Daddy!" Oliver screamed, rushing to the edge of the sidewalk and waving to his father. Ron jumped out of his seat to hold on to the five-year-old so he wouldn't dart into the street.

"Sometimes I still want to scratch your eyes out for taking my first true love from me," Teddy muttered.

"You don't want him," Amanda said. "He's stubborn."

Teddy arched what he knew was a perfectly manicured eyebrow. "Oh, and you aren't?"

"Not like him."

Teddy snorted again.

"You have Adam. He's cut from the same damn Bryson cloth."

Teddy *hmm*'d. "That he is, girlfriend. But…"

Amanda's head spun towards him. "But?" she yelled, catching her husband's attention as he drove by.

Teddy waved a reassuring hand towards Max, letting the man know he didn't need to save his wife from anything nefarious. Except Teddy's woes.

Which he was about to unload on his BFF. "I had a little meltdown this morning."

Amanda's brow lifted and not in surprise. "Little?"

He grimaced. She knew him only too well.

He squeezed his index finger and thumb together just leaving a little space between them. "An itty bitty one."

"There's nothing itty bitty when it comes to you," Amanda reminded him.

"I know, right? *Rawr!*" He made a clawing motion with his hand.

"That's not what I meant."

"But it's true."

"Something I don't need to know."

"But still fact."

"I'll take your word for it."

"Just ask Adam."

"I'm not asking Adam how big you are."

"Why? He'd vouch for me."

"*Aaaaaanywaaaaay…*"

Teddy dropped his voice to a whisper and leaned close to Amanda. Especially since Hannah was sitting on his other side. Most likely eavesdropping. "Anyway, I really think he's having second thoughts."

Amanda gasped. "He is not!"

"Or possibly having an affair," he said under his breath, just loud enough so she could hear him.

Amanda shook her head. "Adam would never cheat on you."

"You don't know that."

"Are you crazy?"

Teddy *shh*'d her to get her to keep her voice down. Which was ironic since he was the one who usually needed to be shushed.

"Have you noticed how loyal Brysons are?"

"He could be different. I'm starting to believe he only accepted my proposal to just shut me up. I think I'm good enough to live with and," he leaned closer and curved a hand around the side of his mouth, to avoid Hanna hearing him, "fuck, but not good enough to be his husband."

"Bullshit."

"Then why has it been so long?" *Oh God*, the whine in his own voice made him shudder. But this was whine-worthy.

"It's not a rush. It's not like you need to hurry and get pregnant because you're past your prime."

"I am not past my prime. I'm only forty-five. And I would love to have his baby. You know he wants one."

"Mother nature hasn't figured out how you can do that yet."

Which might be a good thing, since it would ruin his figure. "No, but that doesn't mean we can't get a surrogate and use Adam's swimmers. But that takes time and planning. We would need to start that process soon."

"You want to use Adam's and not yours?"

Teddy half-shrugged. "I finally got my Bryson buck, now I want that buck's baby. Honestly, I want it to look just like him, not me. Oh, and I could dress him up so cute!" He grabbed Amanda's thigh and squeezed. "Adam has to love me, right? He puts up with all my shit. Nobody would put up with me unless they did."

Amanda smiled and patted his hand. "Yes, he loves you."

"Then he should want to marry me."

"The Bryson bucks always had problems with commitment," she reminded him. "Even Adam."

"But if we're going to have a baby, we need to do it soon. I don't want to be asked if I'm my kid's grandfather," Teddy shuddered, "when I pick him up from school. It's bad enough he'll probably be teased for having two dads."

The clip-clop of horses headed their way, followed by a few other floats from businesses around the area and the high school football team.

He sighed. "Speaking of two dads, Manning Grove needs a Pride Parade."

"Hmm. Yeah. Though, that might end up being a single float parade."

"But I'd rock it." He did his signature two snaps and a clap.

"That you would."

"And you know Adam and I aren't the only ones flying the rainbow flag. I bet a couple of those leather-clad gorillas riding those hot, rumbly motorcycles are, too."

"I doubt it."

"You never know, since men in leather is such a gay thing."

"Depends on the leather. I haven't spotted any of them riding their motorcycles in assless chaps yet."

"Oh. Now that—"

"It would give your blue hairs a heart attack," Amanda said.

"It would be so hot, though. Some of them have really nice tushies."

"I haven't noticed," Amanda lied.

"Mmm hmm."

"Well, if you arrange a Pride parade, we'll walk the route with you." Amanda waved a hand down the line of sitting Brysons. "We all will."

"At least it would be in June instead of this crazy cold weather. *Brrr.*" He hugged his shoulders and shivered dramatically. "Since my man isn't here, I might have to find one of those bearded gorillas to keep me warm."

"I'd stick to hot chocolate, Teddy. Adam isn't the sharing type."

Teddy's eyes lit up. "No, he isn't. I love, love, *love* when he gets all jealous over me."

"See? Proof he loves you."

"Mmm. I don't know why."

"Honestly? I don't know, either," Amanda said in all seriousness.

Teddy's mouth dropped open. "You didn't!"

She laughed. "I think I did."

"Oh! Here comes Du—"

"Santa," Amanda quickly corrected him.

"Oh, yes, right. *Santa*. Santa's beard needs a trim, it's looking a little ragged. I'll have to get him into my chair. He fights me tooth and nail but I'm learning how to tame that savage beast."

"Not until after he delivers the kids' presents, please. We don't want him delayed or we'll hear a bunch of whining tomorrow morning."

"That would not be pleasant."

Amanda gave him a look. "Right. Whining isn't pleasant."

Teddy rolled his eyes. "Unless there's a good reason for it."

"Here comes that reason."

Teddy's head twisted in the direction Amanda was staring.

Adam hoped to hell that Amanda hadn't spilled the beans. She and Teddy were as thick as thieves, but he didn't want to ruin his surprise for his fiancé.

It had been a struggle to keep it secret since Teddy felt the need to know *everything* that happened in the Bryson family, even if it didn't concern him.

Though, in a few days, Teddy would probably be whining about too much sex and also sand in all of his cracks and crevices.

He could see the man wearing a big floppy sun hat, white zinc on his nose, oversized Jackie Kennedy-Onassis sunglasses and sipping a tropical drink with one of those little colorful umbrellas.

And maybe even wearing a banana sling bathing suit.

Hopefully, Adam could talk him out of the last. Not talking him *out* of it, but talk him out of *wearing* one. In truth, it would be easy to talk him out of it. All Adam would have to do is get naked himself.

His future husband was crazy, but it was the type of crazy Adam could deal with. It kept his life from being boring, that was for damn sure.

And Teddy kept Adam's thick eyebrows on point. That was a plus.

As he hit the Brysons' spot on the sidewalk, he stopped at every chair and gave hugs to the ladies, a handshake to Uncle Ron, and hair ruffles to the kids, even Greg, who laughed and jumped out of his seat to give Adam a bone-crushing hug, anyway.

One kid's hair he did not ruffle was Hannah's. She would've squawked like a hen trying to lay an egg if he even tried. So, he stopped in front of the ten-year-old going on sixteen and held out his hand.

Hannah knew the routine. She unburied one of her hands from under the blanket she was huddled under, pulled off her purple glove and placed her hand in his. He dropped to one knee, bowed his head and kissed the back of it. "Good day, Princess."

"Good day, peasant," she responded like normal, lifting her nose and her voice sounding all hoity-toity.

"If it pleases my princess, her peasant would like to pass so I can visit with my fiancé?"

"You may," she said like an eighty-year old queen. A queen of the royalty, not of the drag variety.

Adam got to his feet and tipped his head in thanks. "Your highness is so generous and kind."

Ron snorted beside her. "If her highness doesn't keep her

hiney in line, all her presents are getting thrown into the fire. Or donated to charity."

"What did you do?" Adam asked Hannah as her face began to twist.

"Nothing," she muttered.

"Were you calling your brother a piece of organ meat again?"

"No."

"Yes!" everyone yelled in unison, including Greg.

"Tsk, tsk, Princess. You won't be allowed to attend the ball."

Hannah rolled her eyes, but her lips curled slightly. "I don't have a prince to escort me, anyway. Dad said no princes 'til I'm thirty."

"Forty," came from Ron.

"Grandpa!"

"Okay, young lady, fifty. Keep it up and I'll add another decade."

"You're not my father!"

Everyone froze. No one moved.

That was, everyone except Ron, whose head turned slowly toward his granddaughter. "You're right. I'm not. I'm your father's father, so that makes me the king of this family. All hail the king!"

Greg laughed and boomed, "Grampa is king! He needs a crown! Gramma that means you're... you're the queen."

"*Uh uh*," Teddy butted in. "I'm the queen in this family. No one is usurping that position from me."

No, they weren't. But Teddy's crown just might be a bit tilted.

Adam grinned at his fiancé, who blew him a kiss.

When he moved in front of his future husband, Teddy held his hand out, too. "This queen expects the same treatment, peasant."

Adam chuckled and dropped to one knee onto the cold concrete, kissing his fiancé's hand.

"Oh," Teddy purred. "I like you on your kn— Ow!"

Amanda had given him a good shot to the ribs. "She's ten.

Remember? She's not dating until she's fifty. Let's not give her ideas in the meantime."

"Like you and that buck of yours don't."

"Mom wants Dad to spank her," Hannah announced loud enough that even the crowd nearby turned. Everyone in the Bryson bunch once again froze.

Ron coughed sharply, trying to cover a laugh.

Teddy turned to Hannah as Adam got to his feet. "Get it right. *Everyone* wants your dad to spank them, girl. *Ev-ery-one.*"

"I don't!" Oliver piped up down the row.

"I don't!" Greg bellowed.

"My dad doesn't believe in spanking," Hannah announced.

"Oh, yes, he— Ow! Girlfriend, I'm going to have a bruise if you don't stop it," Teddy complained to Amanda.

Ron turned to his granddaughter. "You don't think your father wasn't spanked?"

"Oh, I'm so jelly right now," Teddy whispered.

"Was he bad?" Hannah asked.

"Oh, please say he was bad," Teddy said under his breath.

"I see I'm only second choice," Adam teased.

Teddy flapped a hand around. "No, of course not. You'll always be my number one. Just like I'm your number one, too, right?"

"Nobody but you, Teddy Bear." And he meant that, even though Teddy was worried about his fidelity right now.

"Aww," Amanda said and elbowed Teddy right in the ribs again, making him wince. "He's so sweet."

"Not always," Teddy responded, wiggling his eyebrows.

"Okay, then, I need to keep moving."

"Yes, you do, handsome. And make sure I have a clear view of that rear as you do so."

Adam leaned over and gave Teddy a quick kiss. He tried not to do too much PDA, especially in uniform, since not all the folks in the area were accepting of his sexual orientation. He didn't want Max to deal with any complaints. Though, the complaints Max had received, after some citizens found out one of their local police officers was gay, were handled quickly and efficiently. His cousin and chief had no tolerance for intolerance.

Max's goal was to build a more diverse department, which was another reason why he was adding Adam's sister, Jet, to the force. However, in the pursuit to make the force more inclusive, more and more Brysons were filling the rank and file.

But after Jet, there were no more Brysons out there who were, or wanted to be, cops. At least until the kids grew up.

After their Aruba trip, or even while on it, Adam planned on having a serious discussion with Teddy about putting into motion the process of having their own child. He knew Teddy was onboard, they just needed to hammer out the details. Maybe after he was done hammering Teddy.

He grinned.

"Oh, I like that grin," Teddy purred.

Adam cleared his throat. The last thing he needed was to sport a hard-on while walking the parade route. "Gotta go."

Teddy flapped his eyelashes at him and gave him a finger wave. "See you at home, lover."

Adam jerked his chin up at him, shared a look with Amanda and headed down the sidewalk, eager for what tomorrow would bring.

He hoped it would be the best Christmas ever. He couldn't wait to surprise Teddy with his gift.

CHAPTER EIGHT

MAX & AMANDA

A few hours after the parade, Amanda sat cross-legged on the bed, rubbing lotion on her hands and elbows. Max was taking a quick shower. They'd eaten dinner and now they were planning on having some adult dessert, since they were still child- and Greg-free.

Make hay while the sun shines was the saying. Amanda was ready to start baling that hay.

She smiled when she heard the water shut off. A few minutes later, her sexy husband opened the bathroom door and stepped out completely naked, his dark hair tousled and damp with his eyes focused on her.

Holy shit, he could still make her all tingly. How did she get to be so damn lucky?

He stopped just on the bedroom side of the open doorway, a wrapped gift box covering his junk.

"What's that?" she asked innocently.

"I'm not sure. When I got out of the shower, it was on the counter."

"Huh. Did it magically appear?"

"Well, it wasn't there when I got in the shower. Do you think Christmas elves left it?"

"Could have been a burglar," she suggested.

"A robber," he corrected her.

"I thought a robber stole things."

"You did. You stole my heart."

"Max!" she yelled, slapping her hands on the bed and feeling a sting in her nose and eyes. "That was so unfair."

He moved closer to the bed, still keeping the box in front of his nether region. He grinned crookedly. "How is that unfair?"

She sniffled. "Because it's Christmas Eve and you're going to make me cry. Get in this bed and open your gift."

He climbed into bed, leaning his bare back against the headboard, setting the box in his lap.

"Well?"

"Take off the lid for me," he ordered in his deep rumble.

"Oh, did you poke a hole in the box and put your dick in it?"

"Would I do that?" he asked.

"Of course you would, pervert."

"Well, I didn't. And I'm no more perverted than you."

That was true. "I don't trust you."

"Well, you're getting my dick tonight whether it's in the box or not."

"Stop screwing around and open it so you can feel guilty if your dick is the only gift you got me."

He lifted the lid and stared down into it. She held her breath until he lifted his ice blue eyes, which were anything but cold at the moment.

He pulled the photos out one by one and whistled softly. "Jesus, baby, you really know how to give a man a hard-on."

"Not any man, just you."

"Well, of course. No other man better be seeing these."

"Just the photographer."

He stared at one of the more risqué pictures, then narrowed his eyes on her. "What?"

"The photographer, of course."

A muscle twitched in his jaw. "The photographer was a man?"

His jealousy was so cute. "Yes."

Max's eyebrows shot up his head.

"A gay man."

Those dark eyebrows dropped back to their normal height. "He'd better be."

Amanda laughed. "Do you like them?"

"Fuck yes," he whispered, pulling the rest from the box and taking his time to peruse each one.

She'd done a sexy boudoir shoot, not knowing what else to get the man who wasn't much into material things.

"You'll have to hide them from the kids, of course," she added.

"I'm framing these and putting them all over my office at the station."

"What?"

"Just kidding. Didn't you just hear me say no other man is seeing you like that?"

"That's not everything, check under the tissue paper."

He glanced at her. "A new sex toy?" he asked hopefully.

Now she regretted not ordering the sex toy she'd been eyeing up. "Just look."

He laid the photos on the bed next to his hip and she could see he was having a tough time pulling his focus from them back to the box. He pulled back the tissue paper and pulled out a small black velvet box. He glanced at her again. "What's this?"

"Just open it!" Her heart was pounding, hoping he loved it.

He cracked the lid open and hesitated for a second before pulling out the wedding band.

He wore a plain gold band now and she wanted to give him something nicer. Something with meaning.

The ring was made of tungsten and the blue brush-finished

center that encircled the ring was fitting for someone so dedicated to his career in law enforcement. The ring had caught her eye and she knew it would be perfect for her husband. While he was not into jewelry, she knew he'd appreciate this piece.

"Look inside the band," she urged.

His nostrils flared a little as he tilted the ring and read what she had the jeweler engrave on the inside. One side had the first names and birthdates of their children. The words were tiny but he'd made them fit.

He looked at her again. "Where's your name?"

"Turn it." On the other side of the band, she had the jeweler engrave: *You're stuck with us ~ A.* Thankfully, her husband had big hands and needed a wide band.

"That I am," he said, his voice rough. He worked the plain gold band off his ring finger and replaced it with the new one. After staring at it for a few seconds, he carefully collected the photos and put them on the nightstand along with the box.

Her husband sat there quietly, staring at those items, his fingers curled against his naked thighs. He was not normally an emotional man, but Amanda could see he was struggling.

She reached out and grabbed his hand, interlaced their fingers and decided to help him by changing the subject. "Where's Chaos?" She was proud of herself when she managed not to sound choked up.

She could see the relief in his eyes when he finally looked at her, and loved that her gift affected him so much. He was so hard to shop for.

"Lying by the fire, warming up his old bones," he answered finally.

"Did you make all the arrangements?"

"I always do everything my wife asks me to do."

Amanda snorted softly. "So, that means you didn't."

"No, I did."

"Then, where is she?"

"We're picking her up from the foster home tomorrow morning on the way."

She squeezed his hand. "He's going to freak."

Max's eyebrows rose and he grinned. "You think?"

"I can't wait to see his face. And you know that will ease the loss of Chaos when that time comes."

His grin dropped. "I'm not sure it will. He's been in Greg's life for almost thirteen years."

"I know. But I hope it helps. Hell, I hope it helps me." Damn dog lived up to his name, but she had fallen in love with the crazy Border Collie. She couldn't imagine life without him. Unfortunately, that time was coming, so they were trying to prevent a massive family meltdown by easing that pain somewhat.

Max cleared his throat. He would have a tough time, too. "Chaos has been around for Hannah and Oliver's whole life."

"Ugh. We're all going to be a mess," she admitted.

"He's got time. He's slowed down a lot, but let's not rush it."

"I'm not. Believe me." She sighed. "Chaos is the face of Boneyard Bakery. He inspired me to start my business."

"He'll be remembered forever if you keep his face on the packaging."

"Why are we talking about this?"

"Because you asked about Greg's gift."

Her lips flattened out. "I've given you yours and we've talked about his, so let's talk about mine next."

"Oh, you think I got you something?"

"Oh yeah, because I left Santa a list."

"The list only had one thing on it."

"Did you notice it wasn't your dick?" she asked.

He laughed. "I did notice you omitted that priceless gem. But, seriously, woman... a new Infiniti SUV?"

"Well, yeah. Haven't you seen those commercials? All loyal, loving husbands buy their sexy, super intelligent wives a new vehicle, park it in the driveway and put a big-ass red bow on the top."

"Sexy and super intelligent? Think about that when you walk out of the house tomorrow morning and see nothing but your old Subaru parked in the driveway. My new wife—the one I'm trading you in for—will be sexy and super intelligent. She'll get the new Infiniti."

She shoved his shoulder. "Hey, those pictures I gave you were sexy."

"Yes, and I bet they took a lot of work," he teased.

That was true. That photo shoot took hours. And that was after Teddy spent forever working on her hair and makeup. Looking naturally sexy was hard work. "I bet you'd buy me one if I got a vagina rejuvenation."

Max snorted. "I like your vagina the way it is."

"Hmm. Those kids did a number on it."

"Yes, they did."

"See!"

"Maybe I got you the rejuvenation instead of the Infiniti."

"*Ooh*. Will it make me a virgin all over again?"

"Last thing I want is a virgin, baby. I love how experienced you are with your mouth... And other things. I don't have time to teach you all of that again."

She laughed. "You never taught me any of that in the first place."

"I gave pointers."

"You did not!" she huffed but smiled. "You're so full of it."

"Full of love for you." He pressed one hand over his heart and winked.

She rolled her eyes. "Oh boy."

"Okay, so I knew you wouldn't be satisfied with just this impressive night stick as your Christmas gift," he said, waving a hand over his now semi-erect cock. "So, I figured I'd sweeten the deal."

"*Ooo.*" Amanda got on her knees, facing him and clapped. "So, what did you get me, my sweet and loving husband, father of the fruit of my loins, my protector and expert lover who ruined me for any other man?"

"I'm glad I did that last one. I saved the male race from you. I took one for the team."

She grinned. "I actually won't argue that."

"What?" His mouth hung open and he put a hand against her forehead. "Are you feeling all right?"

"Depends on my gift. Let's go, cough it up."

"It's not sexy photos of myself," Max warned her.

"Oh good."

"Though, I might have to steal that idea for a future anniversary gift."

"Hurry up, or you won't make it to our next anniversary."

"So bossy," he murmured.

"I learned from the best," she exclaimed.

He reached under his pillow, pulled out a plain manila folder he'd hidden there while she showered and handed it to her.

Her excited eyes turned confused. "You brought work home?"

"Yes, that's what you're getting, budget spreadsheets. Open the damn thing."

She flipped it open and gasped. Her hazel eyes flipped to his. "A family vacation?" She fingered the paperwork in the folder. "Please don't tell me it's to Aruba and we're leaving the day after Christmas."

"Not to Aruba," he assured her. "No, I figured it was time that we take another honeymoon. Just the two of us. One other than staying at the Finger Lakes this time and getting totally sloshed on wine."

"Oh, thank fuck," Amanda said. "You know Teddy is my bestie, but it will be nice to take a trip without drama. Wait... you said just the two of us?" Her face lit up.

Max gave her a smile and wiggled his eyebrows. "No kids."

"Oh, I just orgasmed."

"Great! Now I can get mine and I don't have to worry about you."

Amanda whacked him in the stomach. "Yeah, right. You don't get off that easy."

She glanced at the itinerary. Her mouth dropped open and her head almost spun off her neck. "Fiji?" she shrieked, making him wince.

Once he could hear again, he smiled. "For two weeks."

"What?" she shrieked again. "Two whole weeks?" Her eyelids fluttered and she shuddered. "I just came again."

"Just wait until we're in Fiji. You'll get sick of all the orgasms I'm going to give you."

"I doubt that." She released a happy squeal, tossed the folder aside and fell onto his chest, wrapping her arms around his neck and planting a kiss on his jaw. "Fun, sun, beautiful water and loads of sex. Best present *ever!*"

"Right? We get caught up in our lives, our careers, the kids, even Greg, and I miss out on spending time with just you." Her dog treat business wasn't as stressful as his job, but she worked hard to keep it in the black. Plus, she dealt with the kids and her brother, who would always require a lot of attention. "We haven't had a lot of time just for us. Greg has always been around and always will be. Though, I knew that going into this." He knew with Amanda came Greg and he'd never had a problem with that. He'd known Greg much longer than he knew Amanda.

"I know and I love you for that. I don't know what I would've done without you, honestly." Her excitement quickly disappeared.

He brushed a lock of her auburn hair away from her face. "You were doing fine," he lied.

"Oh, bullshit. You called me irresponsible plenty of times. In fact, you yelled at me for it, too."

"You found your way." Which was not a lie. It took her a bit but she went from a spoiled brat to being solidly grounded. Even though she resisted for way too long, she finally discovered the appeal of a small town.

"Your family helped," she whispered, her fingers walking down his naked chest and beginning to wake up his cock again.

"My family loves you." And that also was very true.

"And I love them."

"Actually, it's not *my* family, it's *ours*. You are just as much a part of them as if you were born into the family."

Amanda snorted softly. "Luckily I wasn't because as our well-spoken, expressive daughter would say, '*Eww!*'"

Max chuckled and then mimicked Hannah, "Yeah, *eww. Gross!*"

She planted her hand on his lower belly. "You know how much I love you?"

He played along. "No, how much?"

She shifted until she was settled between his legs, a naughty smile directed at him. "Do you want me to tell you? Or show you?"

"Both?"

His wife was so fucking beautiful. Those boudoir pictures were special and he'd cherish them, but he preferred her in person. No makeup, no fancy hair style, no sexy lingerie needed. He only needed her.

Forever.

PART THREE

CHRISTMAS DAY

CHAPTER NINE

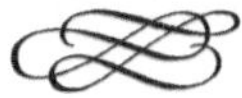

MAX & AMANDA

Max held the door open for Amanda and, as she and Chaos squeezed past him, he grabbed her ass.

"Oh, look at you, old man, last night wasn't enough to wear you out? You better save up some of that energy for Fiji." She had a hard time not running around the house squealing with excitement like one of the kids.

In fact, the kids didn't know yet that they were staying with their grandparents for the next two weeks. If he had told them, her present would never have been kept a surprise from her.

Her kids were horrible at keeping secrets. That was a fact. Amanda learned the hard way when she'd say, "Don't tell your father!" and then they'd go blab to him as soon as he got home.

Tattletales.

Plus, they probably would've moped around the house about not being able to go with them.

Amanda's smile grew to epic proportions.

"You might want to turn down that blinding smile so it doesn't tip off our children."

"I can't," she whispered.

Her husband helped her remove her coat and put it into the

closet along with his. All the presents they had bought, for their own kids and everyone else, should already be stacked under the tree the kids decorated yesterday.

Except for Greg's. The rescue puppy was in a crate in the Boneyard Bakery, since that outbuilding was heated. They had picked her up a little while ago from her foster home and Amanda couldn't wait to see Greg's face when they brought her into the house.

As she went to follow a slower moving Chaos, Max snagged her wrist and pulled her to a halt.

She glanced at him over her shoulder, her brows pinned together. "What?"

"Remember that first Christmas when you were a big pain in my ass?"

"I remember that first Christmas when *you* were a big pain in *my* ass. Always in my business and trying to take control of my life."

"I don't remember it that way."

"Of course you don't. You even told me *what to wear* Christmas day. So, what about it?"

His eyes rolled upward.

So did Amanda's. "Oh."

He jerked on her wrist, pulling her into him. "We had our first kiss under the mistletoe in this very house."

Was it their first? She couldn't remember. Back then she'd had all kinds of sexy dreams about the frustrating man. They most likely kissed in one of those first. "The beginning of the end," she muttered.

"You probably fell in love with me the moment our lips met."

"I don't remember you being drunk that night, nor are you drunk right now, so does dementia run in your family?"

"My parents are as sharp as tacks."

"That they are, thankfully. So, you should remember how I resisted."

His lips twisted. "You didn't resist. I thought you would swallow me whole."

"Bullshit," she whispered as he lowered his head.

"You couldn't get enough of me," he murmured.

"I couldn't get away from you fast enough."

"Bullshit," he echoed in a whisper as he dropped his lips to hers.

He closed the gap and she *tolerated* him kissing her for a few seconds... Okay, like a minute. Or two.

Until they heard the loud, deep clearing of a throat. That got Max's tongue out of her mouth and back into his own, but he smiled against her lips. "If you ignore him, he'll go away."

"That didn't work with you," she whispered back.

"Your children are about to bust their seams waiting to open presents," her father-in-law announced.

Max lifted his head. "Did Mom make breakfast?"

"You should have been here earlier if you wanted breakfast," Ron told him sternly.

Max glanced at this watch. "It's only eight."

"And your children, along with your nephews and Greg, had your mother and me up at five in their excitement to see what Santa brought."

"Is everybody else here?" Max asked his father. They already knew they weren't because they hadn't seen their cars parked outside. But, of course, Max was stubborn just like Ron, so her husband was making a point.

"Not yet. But they're losing one present for every fifteen minutes they're late. Except for Matt and Carly, since they're dealing with an infant."

"We should all get a late pass since we are dealing with your sons," Amanda reminded Ron.

"I'll take that into consideration. Now, your mother made a huge pot of coffee. There's a French toast casserole and a quiche in the kitchen, if you're hungry."

"Coffee and Ma's food or our children, which is more important?" Max murmured in her ear.

"You have to ask?"

"Right. Let's tiptoe to the kitchen, then."

But they were spotted before they could stuff their gullets and get caffeinated.

"Dad!" Hannah sprinted across the living room to her father and glued herself to his front, pushing Amanda out of the way. "I've missed you!"

Amanda's lips flattened out.

Max glanced at her over their daughter's head, shot her a smug grin, then shrugged.

She rolled her eyes. "You know, kid, I'll remember this moment when in six or seven years you come running to me screaming about how a boy is trying to come up the driveway to take you on a date and your father is standing on the deck with a shotgun in his hands."

"He wouldn't do that!"

"Oh, don't you doubt it. And I'll remember just how much you loved your daddy more than me."

"Dad!"

Max chuckled. "We'll see."

Oliver ran up and glued himself to the only space left on Max's body, the back of his thighs and ass, since Hannah wasn't letting him go or willing to share the front with her little brother. "Daddy, you gonna do the same thing with me?"

"Nope," Amanda answered their son. "The second the clock hits midnight on your eighteenth birthday he's going to pack you up in a box and put you at the end of the driveway for UPS to pick you up and ship you out."

"No, he won't!" Oliver laughed, peeking at her from behind his father.

"No, I'll wait until 12:01," Max told his son, running a hand over his messy dark hair. "Were you good for your grandparents?"

He peeled off both children so he could walk into the living room where Ron was now settled in his recliner, sipping coffee with a gray-faced Chaos already laid out at his feet near the fire. Mary Ann was sitting with Greg on one of the couches, with a coffee mug in her hand, too.

Amanda hoped they hadn't given Greg any coffee. Today was not a day for him to be wired out of his mind. There would be enough excitement already.

"Did you drink all the coffee, Bud, or did you leave some for us?" Amanda asked her brother. She needed to know in a roundabout way if she should prepare for activity overload. And if they should all wear bubble wrap to protect them from his flying arms.

"No! Grampa said... said no coffee for me."

Oh, thank fuck. "Good idea, Grampa," Amanda said catching Ron's eyes and he winked at her knowingly.

The front door opened and two miniature draft horses came barreling around the corner, a long string of slobber hanging from Menace's mouth. Both mastiffs plowed past Max and immediately found their little humans, Austin and Jax, who were sitting on the floor engrossed with their tablets. Trouble's big tongue licked up Jax's face, from his chin over his open mouth and up his nose, leaving a path of slobber.

"Guess you didn't use a napkin during breakfast this morning, did you?" Amanda asked the four-year-old.

"Who needs a napkin when you have dogs?" Marc announced as he came around the corner from the foyer to join them. Leah followed behind him, her cheeks pink.

"Did you two walk here?" Mary Ann asked, her eyes narrowed on Leah.

"We were trying to wear the dogs out a little since it's going to be tight quarters today," Marc answered.

Ron jumped from his recliner and went over to Leah. "Come

sit down on the king's throne and put your feet up. I'll rub them for you, if you need it."

"No, Pop, she doesn't need her feet rubbed," Marc growled.

"Yes, she does," Mary Ann insisted. "All pregnant women do. Gets the blood flowing."

"In Leah or Pop?" Marc asked.

Leah rolled her eyes at her husband as Ron escorted her to *his* seat and helped her sit.

"The woman is carrying my grandchild, she deserves to be spoiled," Ron said.

"And she puts up with you," Max added under his breath, loud enough for his brother to hear. "For that she deserves an award."

"Get your wife a plate and some juice," Ron ordered Marc.

"Pop and his harem. Fuck me. If he didn't have Mom, we'd have to hide our women," Marc muttered as he turned and headed toward the kitchen.

They heard the door open again and a loud, "*Yoo hoo!*"

"Uncle Teddy's here!" the boys all yelled and a wild pack of man-children rushed past them to tackle Teddy.

"Oh, look at all these baby gorillas." He came around the corner, fighting his way past them, carrying one small wrapped gift in his hand. Adam followed on his heels, a mile-high mountain of gifts in his arms, so high Amanda wondered how he could see where he was walking.

"Are those for us, Teddy?" Greg bellowed in excitement across the room.

"Some of them, yes. Some are for the adults who will open them in private when they get home."

"Sweet!" Amanda said.

Adam placed the small mountain next to the beautifully decorated tree since there wasn't any room left under it. "Nobody opened gifts, yet?"

"We were waiting for all of you before they tore into them," Ron said.

"Grandpa made us wait," Hannah grumbled, now sitting next to her grandmother, her legs tucked under her and her nose in her phone.

Max went over to his daughter and plucked the phone—one he was not happy Amanda bought her—from her fingers. "No phones today. Today is a day to spend with family, not strangers."

Her mouth gaped open. "They're my friends. And the boys have their tablets!"

Max pulled Oliver's tablet from his hands and then with an approving nod from Leah, took Austin and Jax's, too.

He took all the electronics and put them on a high shelf out of reach. "Grandpa will give those back to you when he decides family time is over."

"Dad!" Hannah wailed.

"Hannah, you aren't going to die without it," Mary Ann said. "Is it so bad to spend some quality time with your family?"

Hannah's lips twisted but she said nothing.

His wife turned to him and whispered quietly, "When do we tell them about staying here for two weeks while we escape to Fiji?"

"We'll send them emails after we leave," he told her, joking but also not.

"Oliver doesn't have email, nor can he read very well yet," she reminded him.

"He'll get the picture when Hannah stomps her foot and has a tantrum about not coming along to the beach."

"When do we leave again?" she asked, when he very well knew, she was aware of *exactly* when they left. She had even put a countdown timer on her cell phone.

He grinned at her. "Like I told the kids, family time first."

"Oh all right," she grumbled, her shoulders drooping and trying to sound like their daughter. "If we *haaaave* to."

"We do. When do we want to surprise Greg?"

"After all the presents are opened and cleaned up. Then everyone will be here. I think the puppy will distract the kids from getting through that motherlode of presents if we don't wait."

"Good idea."

"But before the other thing." She wiggled her eyebrows.

"I agree. Before the other thing. Otherwise, Greg might wonder where our gift to him is and get upset."

Teddy was suddenly there, leaning into Amanda, making them both jerk in surprise. "What other thing, *hmm?* What secrets are you keeping from your BFF?"

Max's eyes hit Amanda's in a silent message and she answered, "No secrets."

"Why has everybody been so secretive lately?" Teddy whined, just like Hannah.

"Stop being paranoid," Amanda scolded him. "Everything is not about you."

Teddy's head snapped up. "It isn't?"

Max sighed. "Do you want some coffee, honey?"

"Sure, *sweetums*, I'd love a cup," Teddy answered with a smile.

"He was asking me. And yes, I do, but I want to grab something to eat while we're waiting for Matt and Carly. I'll come with you."

Teddy made a disgusted face. "When did he start calling you honey?" He followed them into the kitchen, where Adam was already stuffing his face, standing by the counter.

"When he got old and could no longer remember my name."

Teddy nudged her with his elbow. "But he can still get it up, right?"

With no kids in the nearby radius, Amanda didn't bother to

whisper. "Yeah, who cares what he calls me as long as I have that, right?"

"Right!" Teddy said, flouncing over to his fiancé and opening his mouth. Adam dutifully put a forkful of French toast casserole into it. "Yummy. Just like you, lover."

"Aunt Mary Ann sure can cook."

"Her lessons are wearing off," Max said, shooting his wife a pointed look.

"I only took baking and cooking lessons from her to prove Mrs. Busybody wrong, not attract a husband."

"May that cranky old bat rest in peace," Teddy said in a sing-song voice. "Lover, can you cut me a sliver of that quiche?"

"You need to eat more than a sliver," Adam answered. "It's going to be a busy day."

"I have to watch my figure. We're only going to be sitting around and eating today. I'll bloat."

"I have to watch what I eat, too. Somebody needs to look good in a bikini," Amanda said in a low voice.

Teddy spun on her. "*Oooo!* Are you taking a trip?"

"My man is whisking me off to Fiji for two whole weeks of getting drunk and laid."

"What?" Teddy shrieked. "I am so jelly!" He spun toward Adam and grabbed a fistful of his long-sleeved tee. "We need to go with them."

"No!" Max, Amanda and Adam yelled at the same time.

Teddy's well-manicured brows pinned together. "Why not?"

"It's our second honeymoon," Max said quickly. He needed to get the idea of Adam and Teddy joining them on their trip out of his mind immediately, because once Teddy sunk his teeth into something, he usually didn't let go.

Teddy pouted. "Oh... well... fine." He said to Adam, "We need to go on a trip soon."

"I'll look into planning something."

Teddy clapped and bounced on his toes. "Oh goody! Surprise

me, but just make sure it's somewhere tropical and there are loads of sexy men in Speedos," he purred.

Adam shook his head. "Got it. We'll head to Jersey."

Teddy pushed playfully at Adam's chest and the younger man dropped his fork onto his almost empty plate and pulled Teddy into his arms, pressing a kiss into his neck.

"Oh, my man is feeling a bit randy, I see." Teddy wiggled his ass into Adam's crotch.

"I'm picturing you in a Speedo next to a big, hairy Italian guy from New York on a Jersey beach."

"Not even funny. You know I'm not into heterosexual bears."

"Reminder," Adam said, "you shouldn't be looking at any other man but your fiancé."

Teddy made a noise and jerked up one shoulder. "No harm in looking. Just no touching." He turned in Adam's arms, grabbed his face and pulled him into a quick kiss. "You know how sexy I find it when you turn into a jealous gorilla. And, *mmm*, you taste like maple syrup."

"So, eat some breakfast. I'll make you a plate."

"I don't want to spoil dinner."

"Dinner isn't until after—" Adam's mouth snapped shut.

"After?" Teddy prodded.

"Until later," Adam corrected himself.

"We usually eat early," Teddy reminded him. His head swiveled. "In fact, usually Ma has a turkey and a ham in the ovens. Both ovens are off. Is she slipping? Do you think she's getting the old timers?"

"The women have it covered," Max said, hoping that would satisfy his curiosity but knowing it wouldn't. He *was* Teddy after all.

Teddy shot Max a doubtful look. "She didn't ask us to bring a dish like she normally does."

"Baby, if Max said it's covered, it's covered," Adam said more firmly. "Stop worrying your pretty little head about it and eat something now, so as soon as Matt and Carly get here, we can watch Greg and the kids open their presents."

"And I can finally open my present from you."

"That will be later."

"*Ooo.* Not around the kiddies, then. I like the sound of that." Teddy moved away from Adam and leaned into Max, flapping his eyelashes up at him. "How did you like your photos? Weren't they hot?"

"Loved them. Was the photographer gay?"

Max didn't miss Teddy's eyes slicing toward Amanda. But when Max looked her way, her face was suspiciously blank.

"Uh. Yes, he was. Super gay. The gayest of the gay. Even gayer than me." He sang the last part.

"I don't think that's possible," Max said. Teddy had to be sitting at the top of the gay pyramid.

"He hit on me the whole time."

"He did?" Adam growled.

"You were there during the actual shoot?" Max asked.

"Of course I was! I had to make sure her makeup and hair were perfect."

"The photographer didn't help her with the wardrobe? Like making sure her nipples were perfectly placed in the holes where they peeked through?"

"Of course not!" Teddy flapped a hand. "I did." He hugged himself and shuddered as he stage-whispered, "I'm the one who had to touch her boobs." Then he stuck out his tongue and made a disgusted face.

"I adjusted my own boobs," Amanda announced. "I'm perfectly capable of fluffing my own nipples so they perked just perfectly."

Max stared at his wife. If he simply stared at her long enough, she'd spill the truth.

"He didn't touch my boobs," she said firmly.

"Well, if he was gay, it wouldn't matter," Max stated with one cocked eyebrow, watching her face carefully.

"Right," she said quickly. "At the thought of touching them, he said, 'Eww! Gross!' just like Hannah."

"Well, luckily, I don't think they're gross," Max announced.

"As much as your face is between them, I'd say not." She smiled, thinking she won that round.

He grabbed his wife's arm and pulled her to him, putting his mouth to her ear. "If you're lying, you *will* get that spanking you want. Then you'll be lying out by the pool at the resort with the red ass your husband gave you on display."

He could feel the quiver run through her. "Then everyone will know what a bad girl I am."

Well, that backfired as his cock twitched in his jeans.

"You know we can hear you," Adam grumbled, putting his plate in the sink and shaking his head.

"And I am very jealous right now at the thought of Max spanking you." Teddy approached and cupped Max's cheek. "If I'm a bad boy, will you spank me, too?"

Adam cleared his throat.

"I'm just kidding, lover. You're the only man who gets to spank my tush."

"Let's keep it that way. Now, you guys eat and let's get this day started." Adam left the kitchen.

"Why's he in a rush?" Teddy asked. "We have nowhere to go but the living room."

"Maybe he's anxious to see what Santa brought him," Max answered.

"Hmm. Maybe. But I can't wait to see what he got me," Teddy said as he rushed out of the kitchen.

"He's going to shit a brick," Amanda murmured into Max's chest as she wrapped her arms around his waist and leaned into him.

"He's going to shit the Great Wall of China," Max said into her hair, holding her tight. "Grab us coffee. I'll make us a couple of plates and bring them out to the living room. Sounds like Matt and Carly have arrived."

"Hey," Amanda whispered, pulling her face out of his chest.

He stared down at her. *Fuck*, he loved her. He couldn't imagine life without her.

"If I was going to squirt out a third kid, I would make sure it was your sperm that knocked me up."

"I love you, too." He laughed, released her and swatted her hard on the ass as she moved to the coffeemaker. "Just a preview for later."

She glanced at him over her shoulder. "Don't make promises you can't keep."

"That wasn't a promise, *honey*, it was a guarantee."

CHAPTER TEN

MARC & LEAH

Marc sat next to his mother, scowling at his father as the sixty-six-year-old married *grandfather* was on his knees on the floor, massaging his wife's feet. Fuck no, not Ron's wife, Marc's mother, but Marc's wife.

If he was trying to make Marc feel guilty, it wasn't working.

If Leah would have asked, he would have massaged her feet. Though, admittedly, it quickly would have turned into more of an internal massage than an external one.

Leah sighed contently and rubbed a hand over her belly, her eyes closed.

"I guess I missed out on all that spoiling," Carly announced as she came into the room. "I didn't have to go through the discomfort of pregnancy. I just got the spoils."

"Where's the baby?" Mary Ann asked since Carly's arms were full of everything but Levi.

Matt came around the corner from the foyer, a cloth like thingy strapped across his torso with a big lump under it. Marc assumed the baby was the lump.

"What the fuck is that?" Marc asked.

"It's a sling or something. I don't fucking know. Carly got it,"

Matt shrugged, "I wear it. Leah's getting you one. Makes it easier to carry the baby or something."

"I have two arms to carry the baby. I don't need to wear one of those damn things."

"Can we watch our language, boys? It's not only Christmas, but the kids can hear you." Mary Ann scolded, getting up from the couch, using Marc's shoulder for balance.

"Fuck!" Greg bellowed from the floor next to the boys and then laughed.

"And there you go, the holiday is not complete without Greg randomly shouting curse words," Max grumbled, as he walked in with two plates of food, handing one to his wife, who was sitting in a folding chair tucked between Ron's recliner and a second couch. One his parents had to buy once their family began to grow.

Marc frowned. "He hears it all the time between you and Amanda."

"Doesn't mean we want him spouting it randomly."

"Why should today be different than any other day?" Marc asked his older brother.

"Because it's Christmas!" his mother hissed, whacking Marc in the arm and then going over to Matt. "Let me see his precious face," she cooed, pulling back some of the cloth to peek in.

"He's sleeping right now," Matt told her.

"Do you need one of your brothers to help bring in stuff?" she asked him.

"I just need the car seat for now."

"I'll get it," Carly said once her hands were empty.

"No." His mother turned toward Hannah. "Hannah, help your uncle."

Hannah's mouth dropped open.

Mary Ann lifted her brows when the girl didn't move fast enough. "Now. Your cousin will need his car seat."

"But we're going to open presents now."

"Carly," Ron called out. "Can you grab one of Hannah's presents?"

"Grandpa!" Hannah cried out, got to her feet and ran out of the room. A few seconds later the front door slammed.

"Oh, I kind of like that method," Amanda said before shoving a couple slices of bacon into her mouth. "Maybe it'll work for her chores."

Suddenly, Marc's two sons were jumping onto the couch and onto him, Jax's knee hitting him squarely in the nuts. "*Ooof.* Good thing your mom is carrying your last sibling, because I think you just destroyed your chances of having any more."

Austin wrapped his arms around his neck. "Daddy, can we open presents now?"

"Is everyone here?"

"Yes!"

"Then it's up to Grandpa."

Both of his boys' heads spun toward Marc's father. Who, thankfully, got to his feet—albeit slowly and with a deep groan—and stopped rubbing Leah's.

Ron moved over to the tree. "This is going to be done in an orderly fashion and—"

All the kids bum rushed him, even Greg, and started pawing through the presents looking for theirs.

Ron whistled so loudly, Marc winced. But it was effective because all the kids froze in place. "First of all, that was not orderly and you need to wait until Hannah is back."

Greg clapped his hands with excitement as he yelled, "Hannah!"

"I'm coming!" came a shout from the entryway. The door slammed shut again and she hurried into the room, dropping the car seat at Matt's feet as she rushed past him.

Matt picked it up, set it out of the way, and carefully sat on the couch between Marc and Carly.

Carly leaned over Marc's younger brother and whispered with

one eye on Leah, "I brought what you wanted. It's in the diaper bag."

Marc only nodded but his heart began thumping out a frantic beat. He hoped what he asked Carly to bring was the right decision. He wanted to make his wife happy today, not disappointed. He still had time to decide whether to give it to her or just wait.

Ron had all the kids, including Greg, sit in a semi-circle around the tree and, along with Marc's mother, directed who opened what. The joy on his parents' faces as they handed the kids their gifts and watched them torn open was priceless.

Wrapping paper flew everywhere, even covering Chaos, whose black and white tail thumped slowly against the floor as he watched over his three charges: Hannah, Oliver and Greg.

None of Marc's brothers or their wives, or even Teddy, said a word as the kids and Greg took their turn getting a present, opening it while everyone watched and then showing off what Santa brought.

One day the kids wouldn't believe in Santa but for now, they did. Hannah might know the truth already, but if she did, she still acted like the jolly fat man in a red suit who slid down the chimney into a roaring fire at the bottom existed.

And for that, Marc was grateful. He loved seeing his sons be surprised with their gifts. Life was simple for them right now and he wanted to keep it that way as long as possible.

He glanced over at Leah, who now had the recliner in the upright position. Menace sat between her legs and she was petting the Mastiff, but kept her eyes on the activity.

He never expected this to be his life. A wife, soon to be three kids, and two dogs.

Leah glanced over at him, a smile on her face and a sparkle in her hazel eyes. She mouthed, "Love you," and turned back to watch the kids instead of waiting for him to say it back.

Trouble lumbered over to him and flopped into a crooked sit, her tongue hanging out and a string of slobber dangling precariously from the corner.

"They need towels attached to their collars," Matt complained. "Amanda should invent something for her business that's a collar where you can pull out disposable wipes for sloppy-ass monsters like yours."

That wasn't a bad idea.

He stared at his youngest brother, who appeared peaceful and calm. No anxiety, no stress, even with a baby strapped to his chest. "Look at you, brother. Landed a doctor wife, now have a kid, plus a job you haven't gotten fired from yet. Next up is a dog of your own and then you might actually be living a normal life."

"If getting a dog makes us normal, we can skip it," Matt said. "Normal is boring."

"Normal is messy," Marc reminded him. "With dogs *and* kids."

"I'm aware of that. I have three nephews and a niece, remember?"

"You've come a long way since Hannah was born." Marc will never forget the day Matt was triggered after being forced to hold their niece when she was just a baby. His reaction had scared all of them. He'd refused to take his meds or go to therapy, and Max had been close to firing him. The Chief of Police couldn't risk having someone so volatile on the force.

"Took ten years to get this far," his brother said softly, his one hand curved around Levi's rear end in the wrap.

"It was worth the wait," Carly whispered, squeezing the hand Matt had planted on her knee.

Teddy came over to the couch, turned around and wiggled his ass as he sat, managing to wedge himself between Marc and Matt with a loud, "Beep. Beep."

Marc and Matt both sighed and shifted as much as they could, which wasn't much since four adults on the couch was a tight fit. If they hadn't moved, Teddy would have no qualms sitting in Marc's lap since Matt's was full with Levi.

He loved Teddy, but not enough to have the man's ass smashing his junk. And Marc doubted Adam would give his approval.

Teddy wrapped an arm around each of them and said, "I love me a Bryson buck sandwich."

"Whenever Adam gets around to putting a ring on it, are you going to change your last name?" Marc asked him.

"Hell yes! I'll be Theodore David Bryson," he said with dramatic flair as if he was on a stage. "I will not shed one damn tear about getting rid of the Sullivan last name. If Adam hadn't come along and fell deeply in love with me, I might have asked your parents to adopt me just so I could change it."

Marc snorted. "Then Adam would be your cousin."

"There's enough of that incestuous cousin-brother goings-on up on that mountain with that Shirley Clan." Teddy gasped. "Ugh. I feel so bad for blowing Autumn's whereabouts that day. I caused this little bundle of wonder to be born early."

Because of something Teddy did, the Shirleys had spotted Levi's birth mother in town after she'd escaped from them, even though Teddy had no clue he'd done it.

"It wasn't your fault, Teddy," Carly assured him. "You had no idea. It was just bad timing."

"It *was* my fault. But Autumn was so sweet and didn't blame me at all. She even covered for me with her leather-vest wearing gorilla. She told Sig her hat fell off and it wasn't me who tore it right off her so I could see her glorious, but damaged, red hair."

"You only wanted to help her," Carly said.

"Maybe you should keep your hands to yourself next time," Matt grumbled.

"You're right, Matty. I tend to get handsy."

Marc and Carly's eyes met over Teddy and Matt. Today was not a day for Teddy's enthusiasm for life to be squashed by a broody Bryson.

"So..." Teddy turned to him, pasting a half smile on his face. "What did you get Leah?"

"A father who massages her feet. You might just think that's a cheap gift, but it was actually expensive. It cost me my bachelorhood and a fortune in raising boys."

"Your father is quite the charmer," Teddy agreed. "You're lucky he isn't twenty years younger or he'd steal your wives away."

"Mom would crack him upside the head with one of her cast iron skillets if he did."

Teddy's smile was back to being genuine. "She would need a new skillet. You all are so damn hard-headed. Now where is Max going?"

"Probably to get Greg's surprise. Get ready," Marc warned.

"We'll need earplugs," Matt said.

"So many babies in this family!" Teddy gushed. "It's too much squishy cuteness. Like me."

"You and Adam need one of your own," Leah said, as she came over to the couch, Menace following her. When the Mastiff reached Trouble, he began licking the slobber off her mouth.

Matt wrinkled his nose.

Marc stood up to give his seat to his wife, but she just waved a hand. "I'm fine."

"We don't need a puppy," Teddy said.

"A baby," Leah clarified.

"We'd need a surrogate. Do you want to volunteer?"

"Leah is not having your baby," Marc growled.

"Well, technically it would be Adam's. But we would raise the little bundle of joy together."

"Leah is not having Adam's baby," Marc growled again. The thought of Leah carrying another man's baby made his blood rush. If his wife was going to be pregnant, then it would be with his sperm not his cousin's.

"Well, look at you going full-on jealous gorilla, Marc."

"I'm not carrying any more after this one. Sorry, Teddy," Leah said.

The hairdresser sighed. "Well, there's still Amanda."

Marc snorted. "Oh yeah, I'm sure Max would be A-Okay with that idea." His older brother was more possessive than Marc and Matt were.

"She should take one for the homosexual team."

"Have you asked her?" came from Carly at the other end of the couch.

"Yes."

"And?"

Teddy sighed. "She said her hoo-ha has never been the same again, so she's not stretching it out a third time."

"She did not enjoy pregnancy," Carly confirmed.

"Well, if I could do it, I would," Teddy stated.

"If men could get pregnant, there would be no humans left on this Earth," Leah stated.

"Why do I hear my name over here?" Amanda asked, coming up behind Leah.

"Because Teddy has plans to knock you up with Adam's swimmers," Leah answered with a laugh.

Amanda's face twisted. "Oh no. That is *not* happening. My vag was never the same again."

"We already mentioned that," Marc assured her.

"Oh, you were all discussing my vagina? Without me?"

"Why does Amanda's vagina always come up in conversation?" Matt muttered. "I'm surprised she hasn't named it."

"Oh, it has a name. It's—"

"No!" Matt cut her off. "I don't want to know it. Christ."

Amanda smirked. "It's not Christ. Though sometimes Max does scream—"

"No!" Matt barked and surged from the couch, supporting the sling by holding Levi with one arm. "Not today, Satan."

Marc snorted. Carly had both hands covering her face as she

shook. And Teddy's green eyes just volleyed back and forth between Matt and Amanda.

"It's not Satan, either," Amanda announced. "Though, that might be more fitting."

"Well, it looks like we'll have to find an available hoo-ha elsewhere," Teddy announced. "Carly, do you know of any?"

"I know plenty of *hoo-has*, Teddy," she answered. "I'll keep you in mind if one becomes available."

"We need to do it soon," Teddy said, staring across the room at Adam.

"Don't you have a wedding to plan first?" Marc asked.

"We're not talking about that right now," Teddy grumbled.

Marc glanced at Amanda and she only shrugged.

Leah settled in Matt's empty spot on the couch.

"You could've moved over so my wife could sit next to me," Marc said to Teddy.

"Why? She gets you all the time. When do I ever get to cuddle with you, big boy?"

"Apparently, she let the secret out."

"What secret?" Amanda asked.

"About how big I am," Marc said with a grin.

"No, but she did let it slip about your nipple rings," Teddy said.

"That's old news," Amanda announced. "Marc, remember the time you had to call Max to release you from being handcuffed to the bed?"

How could he not? It was the day his secret was leaked to the family about his nipple piercings. He had never lived that day down. "I also remember Max giving me pointers when he arrived about making sure a cuff key was taped to the headboard. Wonder how he knew that?"

Amanda laughed. "Well, of course he knew that. It's Kink 101. You should've known that trick."

He didn't. But it was one lesson he learned the hard way.

But luckily after that, he and Leah had kissed and made up. And now look at them. About to have their third kid.

Ignoring the stroll down kinky memory lane between Amanda and Marc, Leah grabbed Teddy's hand and put it on the side of her belly. "Feel that?"

At first, Teddy jerked his hand away, surprised. Then he placed it back where it was. "*Oooh*. He's a feisty one."

"She," Leah corrected him.

"I thought you didn't know."

"We don't."

"Well, the odds are it'll be another miniature Bryson buck. Ron passed down those strong male genes."

Leah lifted crossed fingers. "I'm holding out hope because of Hannah."

Amanda perched on the couch's armrest, next to Marc. "Hannah's just an anomaly, that's all. She lured us into the false hope that more estrogen could be born into the family to even out all that testosterone. It was a trap."

"There's nothing wrong with all the testosterone in this family. I, for one, am not complaining." Teddy leaned over Marc, waved his hand under his own nose and inhaled. "That alpha scent's an aphrodisiac."

Marc grinned and puffed out his chest.

"Maybe for the adult male gorillas, Teddy," Leah said. "But the baby gorillas are just stinky creatures."

"Just a warning," Teddy said, now leaning into her. "They get worse before they get better."

"Great," Leah moaned. "Another reason to want a girl."

"Do you care what you two have, Marc?" Amanda asked him.

"I want whatever makes my wife happy."

Amanda whispered loudly to Leah. "Ask for an Infiniti SUV. Tell him that will make you happy."

The sound of the front door closing got the adults quiet. Max's heavy boots came in their direction and when he appeared in the open entryway to the living room, he had an armful of a squirming ball of fur.

"I think this is the last present of the day," Max announced, catching the kids' attention. And Greg's.

Everyone ten and under squealed or screamed and ran up to Max, surrounding him and trying to pet the twelve-week-old puppy Amanda and Max adopted from a local rescue. Trouble, Menace and Chaos also rushed over to see what the fuss was about and meet the newest four-legged member of the family.

"Aw, whose puppy is that?" Hannah asked, her eyes alit with excitement.

"Officially? Greg's." Max answered his daughter.

Greg slowly got up from the floor where he was playing with one of the kid's new toys and approached Max. "He— He's for me?" he asked, his eyes rolling, his hands twisting in impossible directions as his arms jerked.

"She," Max corrected. "And yes, she is, Bud. Santa delivered her to us, so we could give her to you."

"I... I didn't ask S-santa for a puppy!"

"You didn't?" Max asked. "Well, then maybe it was a mix-up and we need to give her back to Santa."

"No!" Greg laughed, reaching out to pet the puppy's head. "'Manda, Santa gots me a puppy!"

"I see that, Bud. You get to name her, too," Amanda said from the couch, a huge smile on her face.

Mary Ann called out, "Please don't name her something crazy like Havoc."

Greg boomed out another laugh. "Havoc!"

"That's a perfect name," Adam said with a laugh. "She'll fit right in."

Mary Ann covered her face with her hands and shook her head.

"There you go, Mom." Marc snorted. "You did it. It's your fault."

"Havoc," Leah repeated. "I like it. No worse than Menace or Trouble."

"Or Chaos," Amanda added.

"What is she?" Leah asked Greg's sister.

Amanda lifted a shoulder. "They think she's a mix between a Border Collie and a whosey-whatsit. Which means they have no idea."

"But you got her from the Border Collie rescue?"

"Yes. They had a whole litter." Amanda lowered her voice. "Just in case you want a third dog to go along with the third kid. You can name it Disaster."

Leah turned her head and hid her laugh from her mother-in-law, who scowled at Amanda and complained, "Whatever happened to normal dog names like Rover or Duke?"

When she could manage it, Leah answered Amanda. "I think we have our hands full. Trouble is still a damn puppy at a year old. She chewed up Jax's slippers and then pooped them out in pieces."

Amanda snorted. "Did you try to sew them back together?"

"Unfortunately, my sewing skills are lacking."

Greg was now sitting on the floor with a licking puppy in his lap. Chaos laid by his side, his tail thumping slowly against the floor and accepting licks from the puppy when she got tired of eating Greg's face.

"Chaos has slowed down a lot," Leah whispered to her sister-in-law.

"It's why we decided to do this now." Amanda also kept her voice down so the kids wouldn't hear them.

"Same reason we got Trouble. I know it'll devastate the kids when Menace goes. He's been around their whole lives. Plus, this one," Leah reached over Teddy to pat Marc's knee, "will take it way harder than the boys."

"Hey, I had him before I met you. He was my first true love."

"Yes, he was and I doubt you would have tolerated me shitting in your shoes like he did," Leah teased her husband.

"I might have given you a pass if you did it while you were naked."

"Eww," Teddy screeched, jumping up from the couch and rushing over to Adam. "Hold me, handsome. Your cousin is giving me nightmares."

"C'mere, wife," Marc ordered, pulling Leah closer to him. "Havoc wasn't the last present."

"No, it isn't," Amanda said with a pointed look.

"I'm not talking about that one. I'm talking about the one I asked Carly to bring."

Leah stared at Marc. "For me?"

"Yes…" Her husband lifted his chin at Carly, who got up, dug through her diaper bag and pulled out what looked like a greeting card sized envelope.

After her sister-in-law handed it to her, Leah glanced at Marc, who looked a bit unsure. Pale even.

"What is this?" Leah asked suspiciously.

"It's a surprise."

"Are we going on a second honeymoon? If so, then we should wait until after the baby is born—"

"No."

"Is it the spa gift certificate you mentioned yesterday? I could use some pampering." Ron's strong hands massaging her feet made her want to book a whole day of the same.

"No. But it's up to you whether you open it now or later… Or not at all. I know you wanted to keep it a surprise but I figured today would be the perfect day, if any, for you to find out what we're having."

"You're havin' a baby!" Greg yelled from across the room.

Leah realized all eyes were no longer on the puppy, but on them.

"I meant, what kind of baby," Marc clarified.

"A human baby, silly!" Greg said, his puppy now on the floor, playing tug-of-war with his shoelaces.

Leah felt the blood drain from her face. She was desperate to know, but she was afraid to be disappointed. In truth, like most parents, she'd be happy as long as her child was born healthy. But also, deep down inside, she really, really, *really* wanted a girl this time. She insisted their second dog be female, simply so Leah wasn't the only one in the house. But a little girl...

Not just any little girl. Marc's. Possibly with his dark hair and stunning blue eyes.

She'd be a daddy's girl.

Damn hormones were making her eyes burn.

She flipped the envelope over and over in her hands, staring at it, very aware that everyone was still watching her. After a few more turns, she lifted her eyes to her husband. "Do you know?"

"No, I told Carly not to tell me. I wanted to find out at the same time as you."

"Thank you," she mumbled, a tear threatening to fall from the corner of her eye. She quickly caught it before it did. "It shouldn't matter."

"I know," Marc said softly.

"He or she will be a part of us. That's all that matters."

"I know. You can throw that into the fire if you want and we can wait."

Leah tried to swallow, but her throat was closing up. She really wanted to know but she was scared.

Her finger slipped under the corner of the sealed flap and as she slid it along the edge, she carefully worked it open. Then she paused, still staring at it. "We could choose a name if we know."

"Baby, do it or don't. It's up to you."

Leah gnawed at her bottom lip. It didn't make sense that the kids were so quiet. It wasn't like them. How could everyone be so focused on her and this decision?

She closed her eyes, flipped the flap up and slid out the card.

Marc jerked next to her and she heard his breath catch. Opening her eyes, she read the front of the card.

It's a boy!

Leah stopped breathing, trying to fight back her emotions. One heartbeat. Two.

"Open it!" screeched Carly. It was unlike her to be so impatient.

Leah opened the card and pink glitter went flying everywhere. Inside was large handwritten block lettering.

JUST KIDDING!
This one doesn't have a penis!
Hooray for more vaginas!

Leah slapped a hand over her mouth and Marc yelled, "Thank fuck!"

His mother scolded, "Marc! Language!"

Greg boomed out another, "Fuck!"

Austin and Jax ran over and grabbed the card from her. "What is it, Mommy?"

"You're getting a baby sister," she told her boys through her tears.

"Is that good?" Austin asked, confused.

"It's great. It means grandma will have another girl to spoil when you two are hanging out with grandpa."

Teddy clapped and bounced on his toes, wrapped up in Adam's arms. "It also means we'll have a girl to dress up since Hannah no longer lets us dress her."

Max and Amanda, Matt and Carly, Adam and Teddy along with Ron and Mary Ann came over, each giving her a hug and their congratulations.

Leah glanced over at a grinning Carly, who was now holding

Levi and swaying back and forth. "A penis can't be hiding, right?"

"Well, that's always a possibility, but every time I've done the ultrasound on you, I did not see one."

"And if she had one it would be big enough to see," Marc said. "Us Brysons aren't small. Right, Pop?"

"Right. I—"

"Ron!" Mary Ann squawked. "It's Christmas. That's not a conversation to have today or in front of the kids."

"You heard your mother, no penis discussions on Christmas."

"There's never not a good time to talk about penis," Teddy stage-whispered.

"Penis!" Greg crowed toward the ceiling, making the puppy bark, which, in turn, made all the dogs bark. "I got a penis, too! No vag... ina!"

"Yes, Greg, vaginas are yucky," Teddy told him with a dramatic shudder and a wrinkled nose.

Leah ignored them and leaned into her husband, turning her face up to him. He lowered his mouth and brushed his lips over hers.

"It wouldn't be a Bryson family holiday without total bedlam," she murmured.

"Would you want it any other way?" he whispered against her lips.

"No."

"Are you happy?"

"You, the boys, your family, make me happy. Never doubt that. Finding out this baby's a girl was just the bow on the box. But the gift inside would've been great all the same." She sighed with contentment, one hand on her belly and one hand cupping her husband's stubbled cheek. "It's been an amazing day."

"The day's only beginning," Marc reminded her.

True. One more surprise needed to be revealed.

And it was a doozy.

CHAPTER ELEVEN

TEDDY & ADAM

Adam's stomach churned, his mouth was as dry as the Registan Desert in Afghanistan, his throat tight. And his heart thumped wildly.

"Why do you keep glancing at your watch?" Teddy asked as Adam lifted his wrist for the hundredth time.

Adam still had him pulled into his arms, his fiancé's back pressed to him, the arm without his watch stretched across Teddy's chest, holding him close.

"And why is your heart doing a crazy thumpty-thump, handsome? I can feel it."

"Too much caffeine."

"Are you anxious to give me my present? Is that why you keep checking the time?"

Fuck yes, he was anxious.

His surprise had taken months of planning and secrecy. Of course he was nervous that it could turn into a complete disaster. Teddy wasn't the most cooperative of people. The slightest misstep could create a whole dramatic episode, effectively ruining Adam's surprise single-handedly.

"I'm so happy there's going to be another girl in the family,"

Teddy murmured plucking at Adam's sleeve. "We need to have a serious discussion about what we want to do. I'm not getting any younger, you know."

"We'll discuss it." And they would. He just needed to get through today first. Once they were on their trip to Aruba, they'd have all the time in the world to make those plans. No family or work schedules interfering. A whole week with just the two of them.

Adam couldn't wait. It would be the perfect time to reconnect since the two of them were so busy. Adam had worked a lot of overtime to pay for today's surprise and Teddy was a business owner, so he tended to work long days. Sometimes there were days they hardly saw each other.

Sometimes they were reduced to only having a quickie, because if days went by without sex, Teddy got it in his head that Adam was losing interest or looking for sex elsewhere. Just like yesterday morning's meltdown.

Teddy's parents' rejection, as well as his first lover's, had given the man some deep-seated doubt of believing that real love existed. Now a part of the Bryson family, Teddy shouldn't be so skeptical since they were surrounded daily by couples who were undoubtedly perfect examples of true and lasting love. Even the older generation, like Ron and Mary Ann and Adam's parents, not only loved each other but were still *in love*. And yes, there was a difference.

Both his and his uncle's families were built solidly on love, trust and honesty. Adam wanted his relationship and possible future family to be built on the same.

He hated keeping secrets from Teddy, but the time was quickly approaching when it would be over and he could reveal everything Adam had worked so hard—with the help of his cousins and their wives—to plan.

Now, it just needed to go off without a hitch.

Unfortunately, with the Brysons, there always seemed to be a hitch.

A knock on the door had the dogs scrambling in that direction.

"Somebody's here!" Greg yelled, just in case everybody hadn't heard the loud knocks or the cacophony of excited barking.

"Who's that?" Teddy asked. "It can't be a solicitor on Christmas day, can it?"

"Probably my brother," Ron said, getting up from his recliner, aka throne, by the fire.

Teddy squealed and twisted within Adam's arms. "You didn't tell me your parents were coming."

Adam shot him a hopefully cool and collected smile, even though inside he was shitting bricks. "I wanted to surprise you."

"Oh!" Teddy clapped his hands and bounced on his toes. "My other mom and dad are here!"

He broke free from Adam and rushed after Ron. Adam sucked in a deep breath, trying to settle his nerves.

Max whacked him on the back and laughed. "Just keep your shit together. Otherwise, you'll blow it."

Adam could only nod.

"And Jet!" Teddy screamed from the front entryway at the same volume as a tea kettle-whistle.

Teddy followed Adam's parents, Cathy and Randall, into the living room, with his sister, Jet, on their heels.

"They're not carrying food, either," Teddy announced, "so now I'm wondering if we're all getting Chinese food later."

"We had Chinese last night," Hannah announced. "I don't want it again."

"I love Chinese!" Oliver exclaimed. "I can eat it every night."

"Oh, maybe we can get pizza," Hannah suggested.

"I'm sure the pizza places are all closed today," Adam mumbled, thinking he just might pass out.

Maybe he needed to sit down.

"Did you know that it started to snow?" Adam's mother announced, shooting Adam a worried look, as she walked deeper into the living room.

Was his face as green as it felt?

"Wow, look at that haul under the tree." She went around giving hugs and kisses to everyone, while Adam's father gave out hugs and handshakes.

"I gots a puppy!" Greg announced.

"I see that, Greg! How lucky you are! Are you going to share that puppy with Oliver and Hannah?"

Greg nodded and gave Adam's mother a toothy grin. "Yup."

Havoc was now wrestling with Chaos's thick, bushy tail.

"So, when are we eating, Momma Bryson?" Teddy asked Mary Ann.

Randall spoke up first. "I suggest we go for a walk before the snow gets any deeper. Your trees look great with that light dusting of snow, Ron. I see you've been working hard on keeping them trimmed perfectly. I bet you sold a bunch this year."

"I did. The boys help their old grandfather out."

Randall sighed. "Maybe one day soon I'll have some grandchildren of my own. Right, kids?" He eyed Adam and Jet.

"Right, Dad. But Adam's older. He should go first," Jet quickly said. "I'm just starting out in my career, no time for being a single mother."

"You can find a man, have babies and still work, Jet," Cathy suggested. "It's called multitasking. You don't need to be so single-minded."

"Or another woman, Jet?" Teddy asked, his eyebrows lifted all the way to his hairline. "No one here will judge if you like tacos instead of hot dogs."

Jet laughed and shook her head. "Career first, love later."

"Like Mom said, you can have both," Adam reminded his sister, doing his best not to puke.

"Meh," she muttered. "I can also have my career and lots of sex without any strings."

"Oh, now that's a good plan," Teddy said.

"Jet!" Cathy yelled. "There are children present."

"Hard to miss them, Mom. And if it wasn't for sex, they wouldn't be here."

"Can I have the sex?" Greg asked, holding a now sleeping puppy in his lap.

"Sex is yucky," Hannah announced.

"First of all, how would you know that?" Ron asked.

"Because I see Mom and Dad kissing all the time. It's gross."

"Hey, let her keep thinking it's gross and yucky. Then I won't have to stand on the deck with my shotgun," Max said.

"I want sex, too!" Oliver announced.

Max grabbed his five-year-old's shoulder. "Not until you're twenty-five."

"Dad!" Hannah cried. "You told me I had to wait to date until I was thirty! How is that fair?"

"Life isn't fair, my darling daughter. Best to learn that now," Max answered, his lips quirking as he tried to hold back his laughter.

"I told you fifty," Ron reminded her.

Hannah rolled her eyes.

"Well, there you go. Your father was out ruled by his father."

"Dad!"

Max shrugged. "He outranks us all."

Ron clapped his hands, getting everyone's attention. "And as the supreme ruler of this house, I agree with my brother, we should all go for a walk."

"What? Now?" Teddy whined. "It's cold out. And snowing. And winter. And *brr.*" He wrapped his arms around himself and shivered.

"Yes, now, before we eat," Ron said. "We can work up an appetite."

"We can't eat if there's no food," Teddy grumbled under his breath.

"When have you ever starved around Mary Ann?" Adam asked him.

"Never."

"I told you to eat breakfast."

"I was saving space for dinner." Teddy made his way over to Carly, who was standing by the car seat, where Levi was sleeping. "I can stay with the baby."

"He's going on the walk. I brought plenty of layers for him and we're going to strap him to Matt's chest again. My husband is like a walking, talking furnace."

"Well, that I have to agree with. Matty is very hot. And when he's broody, he's smoldering."

"Everyone bundle up," Adam's dad yelled.

Teddy's lower lip jutted out. Adam approached him and dragged a thumb over it. "Baby, it's just a walk. You aren't going to die. It'll be fun."

"How do you know I'm not going to die? We could be attacked by a rabid pack of rabbits. Haven't you ever watched a horror movie before?"

Adam put his lips to Teddy's ear. "I'll protect my Teddy Bear. I promise."

"Oh," Teddy breathed. "Don't make me hard in front of the children."

"Good idea. Put on your coat and your five thousand winter accessories that are color coordinated and get ready."

"I'll have you know those accessories are vital to my winter survival."

"You live in Manning Grove, not the arctic circle," Adam reminded him.

Teddy sighed and moved with the rest of the family toward Randall as he stood by the closet and handed out coats, gloves, hats and scarves to their owners.

Adam stood back and Max paused next to him, whispering, "We got it from here. Just take a breath."

Easier said than done.

"Okay, let's go," Adam heard his father say in his best retired cop's voice. "As soon as you're dressed appropriately, go outside on the porch. Let's keep this orderly and organized."

If Adam wasn't so sick to his stomach, he'd laugh. Retired or not, you can never remove the cop out of the man.

He purposely stood at the back of the pack. His father handed out the last coat to Max, who waited for Randall to walk outside first. "I'll keep him out," his cousin mouthed.

Adam nodded, pulled out his cell phone and said loudly, "You go on ahead. I need to make a quick call."

"What?" came a screech from outside on the porch.

"You all go on. I'll catch up."

"Who are you calling on Christmas?" Teddy shouted back into the house.

Max shut the door firmly, cutting off Teddy's complaints.

Adam turned and sprinted up the stairs as fast as he could. He was either going to throw up or his heart was about to explode.

He wasn't sure which would be worse.

"I told you something suspicious is going on," Teddy hissed at Amanda as everyone else filed down the porch steps and headed down the snow-dusted stone sidewalk. "Who is he calling on Christmas? Everyone he would talk to on a holiday is here."

Amanda hooked her arm in his and pulled him along. Teddy wanted to dig in his heels, run back inside and demand to know who Adam was talking to.

"It's nobody," she said. "Probably work."

He twisted his neck to glance at Max who was coming up the rear. "Why would he call into work today? The freaking chief is right here with us!" His voice was getting higher the more he melted down.

"Dunn had a question about a case they were working together, that's all," Max said. "Remember, everyone else is working today so we could all spend Christmas together. Dunn did a selfless act by volunteering to work and is missing out on Christmas morning with his family. If he has a damn question, then Adam can spend a couple minutes answering it. Teddy, stop being so goddamn selfish."

Teddy pouted at Max's scolding. "Well, how is he going to find us?"

"He's a cop. He'll find us," Amanda assured him.

"Look down," Max ordered.

Teddy looked down at the ground as the group rounded the back of the house and headed toward a row of trimmed evergreens like a herd of sheep with Chaos circling them, making sure everyone stayed together.

"He's not going to lose us," Max said.

True. With the group they had, there were plenty of footsteps, even in the light dusting of snow. "I should go back and keep him company."

Amanda tugged him along, almost pulling his arm out of the socket. "No, he'll catch up quicker without you to slow him down."

"Fine," Teddy huffed. "If we have to send out a search party... And then we find my Adam frozen like a popsicle..."

"Then, bonus, he'll be stiff forever," Amanda said, yanking him along.

Twenty minutes later, his nose was numb, they were still walking with no end or Adam in sight. He'd texted his fiancé five times with no response. "I don't like this. Someone needs to go back and look for my fiancé."

Everyone ignored his panic, like he was just a silly boy, and kept walking. Like they didn't care that Adam could be found frozen to death amongst rows of Christmas trees or... or...

Having an affair.

A whimper escaped his lips.

"Stop it," Amanda hissed at him.

"He might be whispering sweet nothings into another man's ear right this very minute and *no... one... cares!*" he wailed.

"If he's sticking his dick in another man's ass, I'll shoot him myself," Max growled.

"Oh." That outburst was surprising, coming from Max. "Thank you for defending my honor," he purred and batted his eyelashes at the man.

"It'll be self-preservation. Because there's no way I can listen to you whine like this the rest of our lives."

"Teddy, you need to stop fussing." Amanda also sounded like she was losing patience with him. "Adam is not cheating. He loves you. He's trying to make detective, so he's going above and beyond right now."

"Yeah, what my smart wife said," Max said. "Now, can we please enjoy this walk in silence?"

"Maybe we should be singing some carols while we walk to drown out the yipping coyotes," Ron suggested from up front.

"What coyotes?" Teddy asked in a panic. "See? The coyotes could hunt Adam down and eat him like a snack. Because he is a snack. But he's *my* snack."

"Oh good lord," Amanda muttered.

Teddy cupped a hand around the side of his mouth and yelled, "Adam! Are you out there? Are you lost? I'm here, lover! Call my name."

"Teddy!" Adam's sister, Jet, yelled back to him. "You're ruining a perfectly peaceful winter walk. My brother is fine."

"Did you hear from him?"

Jet rolled her eyes and kept walking. *Well, fine, then, if she didn't give a hoot about her brother.*

Up ahead, Ron waved his arm in the air and the pack hooked a left.

"I'm not sure why we're only walking through rows of trees. That's all we can see. Trees, snow and looming death!"

Amanda jerked his arm as they cut through a couple rows, the snowy evergreen branches brushing against them and sending a cloud of crystals up into the cold air.

As they broke into a small clearing, Teddy stumbled to a stop. Amanda released his arm and moved out of his way so he could have a clear view of the open circle.

His heart began to drum a beat in his chest.

Little white lights, strung in the trees around the perimeter, were lit under the dusting of snow, creating a soft glow, even in the daylight.

Rainbow-colored rose petals were sprinkled on top of the snow-covered ground.

Teddy sucked in a breath of frigid late December air.

Kaleidoscope roses! He had talked about getting them for his wedding bouquet. But they were spread all over the ground instead. Who would do such a thing?

"Oh... my... God!" he squeaked and slapped a hand over his mouth as his fiancé appeared between two snow-covered evergreens. Adam looked as handsome as ever in a well-fitted dark suit with a boutonniere made of a single kaleidoscope rose and tuft of baby's breath.

What the hell was going on?

His lover held a small bouquet of the same colorful roses in one hand.

Teddy tried to swallow, but he couldn't. He was too choked up.

"Did I die on the walk? Is this gay heaven?" he managed to ask Amanda.

"Yes. You made it in," she answered. She lifted her chin towards Adam. "Go claim your eternal reward."

"Is this what I think it is?" he whispered, his voice beginning to thicken as his fiancé moved to stand under an arch made of dried woven vines and covered in twinkling white lights and evergreen boughs.

"It's actually a sacrifice. And we volunteered you," Amanda told him. "There's a pentagram drawn under the snow. Max, grab him so he doesn't escape."

Teddy laughed through the tears that were building and shoved Amanda gently. As she took a step back to catch her balance, he grabbed her shoulders and pulled her into his chest, hugging her close. "You helped do this, didn't you?"

"Maybe," she murmured. "But we all played a part."

"Was this why he was on the phone so much?"

"Yes."

"I never thought it would happen," Teddy whispered.

"I know," she whispered back.

"Adam really loves me."

"Of course he does. We told you that. *He* told you that. You were the idiot who questioned it when no one else did. Now, go get your husband. He's waiting."

He released his bestest friend in the whole wide world and squealed, "Oh... em... gee! I'm getting hitched!"

"Not if you don't go over there!" Amanda yelled at him, giving him a push.

Chuckles rose around the circle where everyone he loved and the most important people in his life stood. Waiting. Watching. Ready to witness Adam and him get married. To commit to each other for the rest of their lives.

To start a family of their own.

Adam was putting a ring on it.

Finally.

Best. Christmas. Ever.

He clapped quickly and skipped over to where Adam stood waiting patiently, lifting the bouquet as Teddy got closer. Teddy snatched it up and put the roses to his nose, inhaling their delicate scent.

They were perfect.

This was perfect.

Everyone in that circle loved and supported them. And it was a bit overwhelming.

A tear slid down his cheek.

"Teddy bear," Adam murmured, using his thumb to wipe it away. "Be happy."

"I am."

"Are you surprised?"

"Floored. You look so handsome and I'm just in these rags. If I would've known, I would've dressed in my best." Teddy waved a hand over his clothes.

Adam rolled his *suck-you-in-and-never-let-you-go* blue eyes. "You're never in rags. And if you would've known, it wouldn't have been a surprise." Adam grabbed his hand and pulled him closer. Teddy, of course, did not resist getting up close and personal with his lover. "I love you, Teddy bear," he whispered.

And didn't that cause another tear to leak from his eye? "I love you, too, lover. I can't believe you pulled this off."

"This isn't everything. I have more surprises."

Teddy's mouth gaped open. "What? More than making me your husband?"

"Yes. But they have to wait. We need to say our vows first."

That sounded like music to Teddy's ears. He was beginning to think this day would never come. It did. "Do you have rings?"

"Of course. I want everyone to know you're taken."

"I want everyone to know *you're* taken." Teddy grinned. He glanced around. "Well, who's going to marry us?"

As if on cue, a portly man with gray hair stepped out from between the trees, wearing a parka over a suit.

"Judge Thomas was kind enough to take some time out of his

holiday to help us out," Adam said. "He's the local district magistrate."

"Are we ready to begin?" Judge Thomas asked.

"Wait! I have one thing to say first." Teddy released Adam's hand and turned to face everyone.

"Just one?" Matty asked, a crooked grin on his face as he bounced gently with little Levi strapped to his chest in the sling.

That reminded Teddy he needed to hurry. Today wasn't only about him. Today was about his whole family. Every single one of them standing around that circle.

"I'm so sorry for complaining the whole time on the walk. I had no idea today's death march would lead me to my little slice of heaven."

Smiles became wider and sniffles louder. Wives and husbands held hands. Kids leaned into their parents. And the dogs played tag with each other through the rows of trees, the newest puppy doing her best to keep up.

If there was one dry eye left at the end of the ceremony, Teddy couldn't tell because everything went blurry for him after Adam declared his eternal love and devotion to him.

Then he did the same.

Teddy was now officially a Bryson.

Someone needed to pinch him to make sure it wasn't only a dream, but a dream come true.

CHAPTER TWELVE

MATT & CARLY

Carly sat on a folding chair near the small makeshift dance floor situated on the ground level of the barn, giving a hungry Levi a bottle. It had been hard work to transform the old barn into a wedding reception winter wonderland. But they had miraculously pulled it off.

The interior was actually breathtaking.

Because the barn wasn't heated, they had rented some portable heaters and placed them around the big, open space. Like out where the ceremony had been held, white lights were strung everywhere, giving the rustic barn a romantic glow. Boughs of evergreens and winterberries decorated the walls. A small lit Christmas tree, full of handmade ornaments made by the kids, sat in one corner, with wedding presents tucked underneath it.

Christmas music played softly from unseen speakers.

Poinsettias had been placed along the center of the long rustic table on a Christmas-themed table runner. They alternated with deep red pillar candles encircled by sprigs of winterberries, emitting a delicate cranberry aroma. The table was wide enough so Teddy and Adam could sit next to each other at the head of the table, while the rest of the family sat down the length.

Another table stretched along one wall, where the caterers were currently setting up a buffet. A two-tiered wedding cake, with two groomsmen standing on the very top, sat on a single table safely out of the way of both dogs and children. One of the figures on the cake topper wore a police uniform, the other a teal tux and pink cummerbund with a leg kicked up behind him as they kissed.

Carly had it specially made and shipped. She'd worried it wouldn't make it in time, but like everything else today, its arrival went off without a snag.

Levi's first Christmas was a happy, but emotional day, for everyone involved. And it wasn't even half over yet. They still had dinner and dancing, along with games with the kids later, as well as picking at leftovers.

By the time they were done, everyone would be exhausted, have stuffed bellies, and be ready to climb into bed and sleep until New Year's.

As she glanced around the barn, she marveled at how far this family had come in the past few years. She might have been the last wife to join the family, but she helped deliver the first Bryson grandchild. And then all the children after that.

Even her own son.

She glanced down at Levi's chubby cheeks as he suckled the bottle, his eyes barely open. He would fall asleep soon with a full belly while everyone else got to fill their own.

She hardly had time to eat this morning, so she was starving, and the food that the caterers were putting out smelled and looked delicious. The table was full of Teddy and Adam's favorites.

For such a cozy and private wedding, Adam had spared no expense. How he pulled it off so Teddy—who liked to be in everyone's business—didn't find out, was another miracle.

A miracle just like her son.

Levi's eyelids were now shut and even though his little Cupid's bow shaped lips were still moving, he was finished. She put the bottle down and before she could burp Levi, Matt was there, carefully taking him from her arms and putting the baby against the towel on his shoulder he'd pulled from the diaper bag.

"I got it. We're about to eat."

Her stomach growled in response.

He grinned at the sound and walked away with their son, patting him gently on the back, moving away from the noisy table where everyone was taking their seats.

Unlike most receptions, seats weren't assigned except for where Teddy and Adam sat. Her father-in-law pulled out the chair at the other end of the table for her, so she would have space on the floor to her right to keep Levi close in his car seat.

"Why are we all sitting down when we'll just have to get back up to grab grub?" Marc asked, taking the end seat across from Carly so that he and Leah had their young boys, Austin and Jax, between them.

"Because we're going to make a toast before everyone starts stuffing their traps." Ron took the seat to Teddy's right and Randall took the seat to Adam's left, with Cathy and Mary Ann sitting next to their husbands. Almost like the parents of the bride and groom. Or groom and groom.

Hell, Teddy wouldn't mind being considered the blushing bride. More like a bubbly one. He was surprisingly quiet during the ceremony but once they said their "I dos" and the two practically ate each other's faces off during the kiss, he was back to his bubbly, outspoken self.

Of course, he made sure everyone saw the matching wedding bands Adam picked out for them at least three times. Just in case they weren't paying attention the first two.

Teddy and Adam were adorable together, though she doubted Adam would approve of that description with him being a Bryson, a Marine and a cop. A triple alpha threat like the rest of the Bryson males.

Her own triple threat put the portable car seat down next to her and took his own seat just in time for Ron to stand and announce, "Since I'm the most senior here, I'm going to start, then anyone else who wants to say something can. If anyone doesn't like that, they can file a complaint with the complaint department, which is a department of one. Me. I'll make sure to take the time to read that complaint before I throw it into the fire. Now lift your glasses."

All the adults, except for Leah, lifted their champagne, while the kids, Greg and Carly's sister-in-law lifted their sparkling cider for a toast.

Then everyone got choked up as Ron obviously struggled with getting his words out. He cleared his throat a couple times, while Mary Ann squeezed his arm and wiped at her own eyes. "We had three sons, so I never thought we'd have a fourth wedding. Because, if nothing, the Brysons are stubborn and loyal, meaning the women that married us are stuck with us forever. We take 'til death do us part very literally. So, there will never be a second wedding for my boys. They found the loves of their lives, the mothers of my grandchildren, and I couldn't be happier.

"But, in truth, we don't have three sons. We proudly have four. Someone left the front door open a crack and another one wiggled his way inside. Once he did, we embraced him as our own. And we're not giving him back. Even though he thinks today is the first day of being a Bryson, that's not true. He's been a Bryson for a long time now. So, I'm not welcoming him into the family because he's been planted in the middle of it for years."

Teddy had a hand covering his mouth and Adam had an arm over his husband's shoulders and wore a crooked grin as he tried to keep himself together.

The women were crying, the men occasionally clearing their throats roughly, the kids not understanding the fuss since Teddy had always been a part of their lives. He'd always been Uncle Teddy.

Ron lifted his flute a little higher. "Cheers and congratulations to the new Mr. and Mr. Bryson." He took a sip of his champagne and everyone followed suit. "I said enough, now I pass it over to my brother." Ron frowned. "Who is now also an in-law?" He shook his head. "I don't want to know." He sat and Mary Ann leaned in to kiss his cheek.

Randall stood and lifted his glass. "Then I will welcome him to *my* family." He turned to face Adam and Teddy. "I have to say, when the two of you literally came out of the closet together at Marc and Leah's wedding, I didn't think it would last since you two are such opposites. But here you are. And today, I gained another son. I also have to say, Teddy, you are one of the best gifts Adam has ever given us."

Laughter rose from around the table and Teddy blew kisses at his new father-in-law.

"Okay, that's it. I'm not good with speeches. Congratulations! And can we all agree that you two need to get moving on giving us our first grandchild? We have a long way to catch up with my brother."

Two seats down from Carly, Jet dropped her dark head, shook it and groaned.

"Get used to it," Carly, Leah and Amanda warned her, all at the same time. The three women laughed.

"Anyone else want to say anything?" Ron asked.

As one, the adults rose, lifted their glasses high and Max yelled, "To Teddy for finally nabbing his Bryson buck!" They laughed as they took another sip from their flutes.

"Yay!" Teddy shouted, clapping and doing a wiggle in his seat. He lifted his hand up over his head. "Has everyone seen my ring yet?"

Amidst the groans, Greg yelled, "Need to eat! I'm hungry!"

Carly was surprised nobody was crushed in the rush to get to the buffet and away from Teddy's flapping hand.

"You stay here with Levi. I'll grab you a plate."

She smiled up at Matt as he planted a kiss on her forehead and went to get in line.

If someone had said the grumpy asshole cop who responded to her car versus deer crash would turn out to be the best husband in the world, she would've argued with them.

And she would've been wrong.

***

"When do you start?" Matt asked Jet as she stood back, watching some of their family moving around the dance floor to a slow song.

Max was dancing with Hannah. Cathy was dancing with Greg. Amanda with Oliver, Randall with Teddy and Adam had grabbed Carly. Leah attempted to dance with a four-year-old Jax, while Marc danced with their six-year-old, Austin.

Ron and Mary Ann moved slowly around the dance floor, holding each other tightly. His parents wore very contented smiles.

"After the new year," she answered. "I look forward to working for Max. And I'm super grateful he offered me the position."

"It isn't a huge department," he warned her, something she already knew but he wanted to make sure she knew she might not have a lot of opportunity for advancement. Not like a bigger department in one of the cities.

"It's not as small as the one I'm working at now. I'm the only female and the men don't respect me at all."

"Sounds familiar," Matt grumbled as he stared at his brother Marc, who used to believe women didn't belong in uniform. Then Leah proved him wrong.

Matt rode with Leah on countless shifts and trusted her completely as back up. In fact, he preferred riding with her rather than a couple of the newer officers they now had on the force. Once he was discharged from the Marines and wore the

Manning Grove PD uniform again, Matt and Leah got close and stayed that way. They had an easy, comfortable relationship both on and off the job. He was glad Marc finally got his shit together and saw her for the good cop she was and then made her his wife.

Marc couldn't have picked a better woman to deal with his goofy ass. But then, neither could he. Carly was perfect for him. Someone solid to grab onto when things were twisting inside him like a tornado.

Amanda was also perfect for Max. His older brother could be a bossy asshole sometimes, and Matt's sister-in-law knew just how to knock her husband down a few pegs.

"They call me every offensive name they know for a lesbian."

"To your face?" To her face or not, they shouldn't be calling her names at all. He felt his blood begin to simmer.

"No, when they don't think I can hear them."

"Wait, you're not one, right?" Because if she was, that was news to Matt. But then, he didn't know Adam was gay until just a few years ago when he hooked up with Teddy at his brother's wedding.

Jet laughed. "No, but dealing with those jackasses makes me want to swear off men."

"Yeah, we can be assholes." Carly called him an asshole all the time in the beginning. And he couldn't argue that. He had been. So, he had owned it.

"No shit. I just worry about them backing me up when it comes down to it."

"Yeah, you have to trust your brothers in blue. Or sisters in blue," he corrected quickly. "Max is a great chief. He was born to lead," Matt admitted. "He doesn't put up with any bullshit. Not from anyone about Adam, not about Leah, either. But then, he runs a tight ship."

Jet glanced up at him in relief. "That's good to hear. Maybe when he retires, one of us will take that spot." A long, dark strand had escaped her ponytail and was stuck to her cheek. She tucked it back into place.

"Maybe one of you younger officers. Not me. I'm good with being in the trenches."

Jet peeled back the fabric of the sling to peek at Levi's sleeping face. "Do you plan to adopt any more kids?"

Matt stared at his son. "I don't think so. We were just lucky Levi came along when he did. Carly happened to be in the right place at the right time. Like it was meant to be."

Fate whispered through his mind.

"Is she in his life?" Jet asked. "The birth mother, I mean."

"Autumn stayed local and, believe it or not, still supplies Levi with breast milk." Matt lifted a hand at Jet's puzzled expression. "That was her decision since I think it helps her deal with the whole situation. But she hasn't been around him since he was born. I think it's too fresh right now. She needs to do a lot of healing first. But we kept that option open to her."

Jet stared at the bottle of beer in her hand. "I heard that whole situation was messy."

"It was."

Messy didn't even describe it. And Matt still didn't know everything that had gone on. He was afraid if he heard it all, he'd go right up that mountain, do something stupid and screw up his life.

Landing in jail for losing his shit on that crazy clan would not help his family. Levi and Carly needed him.

Hell, he needed them.

Which meant, it was best he didn't know all the details. Autumn was now living a better life and Levi was healthy and loved. That was all that mattered at this point.

"Somehow she got mixed up with the Shirley Clan living on that mountain. We'll make sure you get the whole lowdown on them long before you start your first solo shift. You have to keep an eye out on those fuckers since they hate anything to do with the government. Hell, they think they're above the law. As long as they stay up on that mountain, we usually leave them alone."

Jet's crystal blue eyes narrowed on him. "You don't think I'll have a run-in with them?"

"Oh no, I *know* you'll have a run-in with them. Guaranteed. We all get that pleasure. You just need to know who and what you're dealing with when you do."

"It'll be nice to be in a department where the other officers have my back."

"Glad you're joining us." And that was true. Jet had always been a no-frills female, more of a tomboy growing up. She could probably hold her own in a struggle with a subject. "You got a place to stay yet?"

"No, but your parents said I could crash with them for as long as I'd like. I might take them up on that for a while."

"That sounds like a good plan. Leah lived with them at first, too, and she wasn't even related."

"And now she is."

"And now she is," Matt repeated as he watched his wife approach them.

"Can I steal my men away?" Carly asked Jet.

Matt's cousin laughed softly. "Yes, we were just talking shop anyway, which we shouldn't be on Christmas day."

"Yes, it's a day off. Enjoy it," Carly murmured. She turned to Matt. "Dance with me, husband."

"My wife is a bit bossy," Matt whispered to Jet like it was a secret.

"Then she fits right in with the rest of us Brysons."

"That's for fucking sure," he grumbled, then shot Carly a big smile.

His wife rolled her eyes at him, but smiled and held out her hand.

"Do you want me to hand off Levi to Mom so we can do some dirty dancing?"

Carly laughed. "No, we can do some dirty dancing later in private. If he's sleeping, leave him in the sling."

Matt nodded and took her hand. She led him out to the tiny dance floor and then turned to face him.

"Hey, beautiful wife," he whispered.

"Hey, handsome husband."

Carly wrapped her hands around his neck, careful not to squish Levi between them.

"You know I can't dance," he warned her. "So, watch your toes."

"We're just going to shuffle."

"I can shuffle."

"Matt..." She tilted her head as she stared up at him. Her smile gone.

Was he the cause of it? What did he do now? Did he do something he wasn't aware of? "What's wrong?"

"Nothing's wrong. Everything is right," she whispered.

He leaned over, trying not to crush the baby, and pressed a kiss to her lips. "Thank you for making everything right in my world."

"I'm not the only one responsible for that," she said softly.

"I know, but you're a big part of it."

"Everyone had a hand in it, including you. And we talked about this yesterday. Let's have only happy thoughts today."

"You make me happy," he told her.

She squeezed the back of his neck as they shuffled slowly in a circle. "Same." She shifted to his side and pressed her forehead to his shoulder as they continued to move in their little bubble.

He closed his eyes, feeling the weight of his son against him as he held his wife, thinking about the only thing that mattered.

Family.

Not money, not material things.

Family.

He couldn't have a better one. He couldn't have one more accepting than they were. None more loving or supportive.

And because of that, he was the richest man in the world.

EPILOGUE

RON & MARY ANN

Mary Ann shuffled into the living room, wearing the new housecoat and slippers some of the grandchildren bought her for Christmas and carrying two mugs of chamomile tea. Her husband sat by the fire in his recliner, wearing new plaid pajama bottoms and a worn snug white T-shirt that showed off how fit he still was, even after all these years.

"Are the kids asleep?" she asked.

Hannah, Oliver and Greg were the only ones staying overnight, since Max and Amanda were leaving in the morning for their second honeymoon in Fiji. They decided it was easier to just let the kids stay tonight instead of dragging them back over in the early hours of the morning.

The house would be full for the next couple of weeks. Especially once Jet moved in. Mary Ann looked forward to having another woman in the house, even if it was only temporary.

"Totally wiped out. All sawing logs right now."

"So is Chaos." She glanced at the Border Collie stretched out in front of the low burning fire, his feet twitching with doggy dreams. The puppy, Havoc, was crashed in a crate in the corner.

These kids with their crazy dog names... She swore they did it just to give her heartburn.

She studied her husband as she approached him. Even in his sixties, the man was still something to look at. The best decision she ever made in her life was saying yes when Ron bugged her to go on a date all those years ago. She eventually agreed when he played her heartstrings by saying he was a Marine about to be shipped out. She didn't think their couple of dates would go anywhere, but they sure ended up going somewhere.

Three sons, three daughters-in-law, Greg, and Teddy. And the grandchildren she always wanted once her sons had become responsible adults. A full life created with a loving, loyal husband who was completely dedicated to her and his family.

She couldn't ask for more.

She held out one of the mugs, but he shook his head and said, "Put it down for a minute."

"It'll get cold."

"You don't need tea to keep you warm. Put it down."

"Is my husband making demands?" she asked with a slight smile and a raised eyebrow.

"Tonight he is."

The second she set down the mugs, Ron grabbed her arm, ordered, "C'mere, woman," in a sexy growl and pulled her sideways into his lap.

She bit back her squeal as to not wake the kids or the puppy. "Ron, I'll crush you."

"No, you won't. I'm tougher than that."

She patted his chest. "You are a tough old bird." She snaked an arm around his neck, pressing a kiss to his rough cheek, which now sported a shadow of stubble. Being a retired cop and Marine, her husband usually kept himself clean-shaven, but when he let his beard grow for a day or two, she had a hard time letting him out of bed.

Not that it was a struggle to keep him there. Ron had always been a passionate man and he passed that on to his sons. His sexual prowess, among other things, helped keep their marriage strong all these years.

However, they kept that fact from their children, since the boys didn't like the truth about how they ended up on this Earth. They preferred to believe they were delivered by a stork.

She sighed softly as Ron dropped his head, a gleam in his crystal blue eyes, and brushed his lips against hers. He deepened the kiss and soon Mary Ann knew exactly what his growing intentions were.

"We have children in the house," she breathed against his lips.

"And we perfected the art of being very quiet when the boys lived here."

"Leah, too."

He chuckled. "Yes, when Leah lived here, too. Marc's head would probably spin right off his neck if he knew his parents were getting it on only two doors down from his future wife."

She huffed. "Like the boys never had sex in this house. Or the barn."

"Or boned in the Boneyard Bakery. I caught Marc and Leah in there once."

Mary Ann grinned. "Hannah might have been conceived in there, too." She pressed a hand to his chest. "What a perfect day. I thought my heart would burst being surrounded by the family we created and seeing how much they love each other. We're very lucky."

"Yes, we are. Now you can stop worrying about Matt."

"I don't—"

"Bullshit, woman," Ron said. "Don't lie to me. No one knows you better than I do."

Mary Ann pressed her forehead to his jaw and stroked his chest. "Well, do you blame me for worrying?"

No, he didn't. He'd spent many sleepless nights worrying about his youngest son. *Hell*, worrying about them all, but especially Matt.

Ron and his brother had both been pressured into following their father's footsteps. So, they did.

It might not have been the worst decision: to enlist and then become police officers since it provided both his and Randall's family a good life.

But he had refused to do the same with his own sons. He'd left it up to them to decide their life's path and would've supported them even if they hadn't taken the same road. Randall let Jet and Adam decide for themselves, too.

Even so, Ron would have shouldered the guilt if any of his sons hadn't come home. While Matt did come home eventually, he didn't come home whole.

So, yes, that particular guilt ate at him. Even years later. As it did Mary Ann, who thought Matt staying away was her fault.

Which was far from the truth.

Age and wisdom, plus a lot of therapy, showed their youngest son differently. And now Matt was creating his own family, just like Max and Marc did.

Ron couldn't be prouder of his sons. They worked hard and loved even harder. He only hoped the next generation did the same.

"You got everything you've always wanted." He turned his head, pressed a kiss to his wife's soft cheek and slid his hand down her thigh to her knee, where he let his thumb sweep back and forth over the fabric of her housecoat.

"I got more than I'd ever wanted. I now have daughters. I have grandchildren. I have you. Even though it was nerve-wracking and still is, I couldn't be any prouder that our boys followed in their father's footsteps."

"And my father's," he reminded her.

Mary Ann pressed a hand over his heart. The heart that would always beat for her. "It's in the blood."

"We'll see what the boys do when they get older."

She released a soft sigh. "To be honest, I won't be upset if they don't join the military."

With the way things were in the world, Ron wouldn't be upset, either.

"They could go to college, instead," she suggested.

"Our boys did good, honey. They served their country and now serve their community. I'm extremely proud of them."

"I know you are. But our grandbabies should follow their own dreams. If they want to serve and then wear a badge, that should be up to them. Not us. Not Marc, Matt or Max."

Ron squeezed his wife's knee, then ran his palm up the inside of her thigh until he found her heat and cupped it gently. "If they're happy, I'll be happy."

Mary Ann wiggled in his lap. "Feels like someone else is getting happy. I think you're about to make your wife happy, too."

"You're not too tired?" he teased, before brushing his tongue along the outer edge of her ear.

"It's been a very long day and you know the kids will get us up early again."

"Then I'll get up with them and let my wife sleep."

"Oh... Sounds like you're in negotiations."

He arched an eyebrow at her. "Do I need to negotiate?"

She giggled, reminding him of when they first met, when they were barely nineteen and twenty years old and they shamelessly flirted with each other. It took him asking her a half dozen times until she agreed to go to the movies with him.

But then, he always liked a good chase.

Somehow with Mary Ann, he was the one who got caught.

Hook, line and sinker.

And once he was, he didn't fight to get free. He only held on to the hook even tighter. He couldn't imagine life without her by his side.

Now here they were, almost forty-six years later and still deeply in love. Not too many couples could say that and mean it.

They were lucky they also got to watch their sons fall into the same forever type of love. He only hoped they were around long enough to see the same happen for their grandchildren.

"I'd carry you upstairs but if I pull my back, I might not be able to take care of my woman's demanding and insatiable needs."

"If you carry me upstairs and lose your balance, we might both tumble back down and break a hip."

He laughed. "That, too. So, how about if I just hold my wife's hand and escort her up to my lair?"

"How about if I just invite my husband into mine?"

"Your husband is agreeable with that scenario," he announced.

"I know he is. I can feel the evidence."

"Then let's not waste that opportunity."

She climbed out of his lap. "Let's go, old man."

She squeaked as she turned to head toward the stairs and he smacked her ass. But before she could walk away, he grabbed her hand and stopped her, spinning her back toward him.

"Second thoughts?" she teased.

"Never with you," he murmured and dropped his head until her breath whispered across his lips. "Like always, I have one more thing to say."

She rolled her eyes.

"Thank you for all you've given me."

"Ron..." she whispered, her eyes instantly turning shiny.

"I hope we have forty more Christmases together."

Her fingers fisted his T-shirt. "Me, too."

"I love you."

She tipped her head toward the steps. "Let's go upstairs and you can show me how much."

"I doubt I'll last long enough for that, but I'll do my best."

She closed the slight gap between them, giving him a quick kiss. "You always do, Marine."

"*Oorah*," he whispered and followed his wife upstairs.

But then, he'd follow her anywhere.

Even to the ends of the Earth.

Semper Fi ~ Always Faithful

I hope you enjoyed revisiting with the Brysons. This is not the last you'll see of them. They occasionally appear in my newest series, Blood & Bones: Blood Fury MC, which is also based in a small Pennsylvania town named Manning Grove.

Turn the page to read the first chapter from Blood & Bones: Trip (Blood Fury MC, book 1)

Thank you for reading A Bryson Family Christmas. If you enjoyed this story, please consider leaving a review at your favorite retailer and/or Goodreads to let other readers know. Reviews are always appreciated and just a few words can help an independent author like me tremendously!

BLOOD & BONES: TRIP (BLOOD FURY MC, BK 1)

**Turn the page for a sneak peek of
Blood & Bones: Trip
Blood Fury MC, book 1**

This series not only takes place in Manning Grove, PA, it includes cameos of the Brysons throughout.

BLOOD & BONES: TRIP

BLOOD FURY MC, BOOK 1

*"Sometimes you have to burn yourself to the ground
before you can rise like a phoenix from the ashes." ~ Jens Lekman*

Prologue
Turn the key

Trip stood in the middle of the deserted building, shaking his head, wondering if it was worth the fucking hassle to start the club back up. To reclaim its territory.

But what other fucking choice did he have?

He'd already had it set in his mind, not only to do it, but to do it right this time.

He wouldn't let his father's club, which died a violent death, just remain a memory. And a bad one at that.

But now that he had done his time in the Marines, done his time in prison, he needed something.

Because he had nothing.

Except his granddaddy's run-down farm, a barn full of farm equipment he had no clue how to use and didn't want to, and the

223

abandoned warehouse he was currently standing in on the outskirts of town.

While he was in prison, his lawyer had shown up and read him his granddaddy's will.

Yeah. He got everything.

Sig got nothing.

Trip was sure his brother wasn't happy about that, if he even knew.

But most likely Granddaddy had made up the will when Trip was still doing time in the service and not doing it behind bars. Unlike Sig who had been in and out of county jail, or the state pen, off and on since he turned eighteen.

But now here he stood. In an empty building, feeling fucking overwhelmed. But still, it was something.

And something was better than nothing.

He also had new ink on his back and an old cut in his hand.

The leather was worn, the rockers and patches on it dirty. All except one.

One rectangular patch on the front had been torn off by his own fingers after using the point of his buck knife to loosen the threads. The patch that used to say "Buck" was now replaced with one that said "Trip." But above it, the patch that had deemed Buck as president remained. That now belonged to Trip.

He'd also used that same knife to remove the 1% diamond patch off the back. He wouldn't need that one anymore.

The club used to be outlaw. But Trip was determined to keep it above board. For the most part.

He'd spent many a night down in Shadow Valley talking with the members of the Dirty Angels MC, soaking up everything their prez named Z told him. Learning how to rebuild Blood Fury stronger than ever. How to keep the money flowing into the club's coffers.

One way to do that was to keep the members out of prison and, even better, keep them breathing.

Dead or incarcerated members weren't any good to a club.

And there had been too many of those in the Blood Fury MC in the past. It had been its downfall.

Trip didn't want that mistake to happen again.

So, they had to play the game. Keep shit on the up and up as best as they could. Become a powerful force, strong enough to withstand the occasional bump in the road.

He had no fucking clue how he was going to pull it off, but he would take the advice he was given and do his fucking best.

He scrubbed a hand through his long hair before tucking it up under his baseball cap, blowing out a loud breath and shrugging on his cut.

His cut.

It wasn't his father's any longer.

This club was no longer his father's, either.

This world, even as broken as it was, now belonged to Trip.

It was his and he wouldn't let anyone destroy it again.

The Fury was about to rise once more. This time stronger and smarter.

**Get Trip and Stella's story here:
mybook.to/BFMC-Trip**

<u>Only Him</u> *

<u>Needing Him</u> *

<u>Loving Her</u> *

<u>Temping Him</u> *

<u>Down & Dirty: Dirty Angels MC Series</u> ®:

<u>Down & Dirty: Zak</u> *

<u>Down & Dirty: Jag</u> *

<u>Down & Dirty: Hawk</u> *

<u>Down & Dirty: Diesel</u> *

<u>Down & Dirty: Axel</u> *

<u>Down & Dirty: Slade</u> *

<u>Down & Dirty: Dawg</u> *

<u>Down & Dirty: Dex</u> *

<u>Down & Dirty: Linc</u> *

<u>Down & Dirty: Crow</u> *

<u>Crossing the Line (A DAMC/Blue Avengers Crossover)</u> *

<u>Magnum: A Dark Knights MC/Dirty Angels MC Crossover</u>

<u>Guts & Glory Series</u>

(In the Shadows Security)

<u>Guts & Glory: Mercy</u> *

<u>Guts & Glory: Ryder</u> *

<u>Guts & Glory: Hunter</u> *

<u>Guts & Glory: Walker</u> *

<u>Guts & Glory: Steel</u> *

<u>Guts & Glory: Brick</u> *

<u>Blood & Bones: Blood Fury MC</u>®

<u>Blood & Bones: Trip</u>

<u>Blood & Bones: Sig</u>

<u>Blood & Bones: Judge</u>

Blood & Bones: Deacon

Blood & Bones: Cage

Blood & Bones: Shade

Blood & Bones: Rook

Blood & Bones: Rev

Blood & Bones: Ozzy

Blood & Bones: Dodge

Blood & Bones: Whip

Blood & Bones: Easy

<u>COMING SOON!</u>

Blue Avengers MC™

Everything About You (A Second Chance Gay Romance)

ABOUT THE AUTHOR

JEANNE ST. JAMES is a USA Today bestselling erotic romance author who loves an alpha male (or two). She was only thirteen when she started writing and her first paid published piece was an erotic story in Playgirl magazine. Her first erotic romance novel, Banged Up, was published in 2009. She is happily owned by farting French bulldogs. She writes M/F, M/M, and M/M/F ménages.

Want to read a sample of her work? Download a sampler book here: BookHip.com/MTQQKK

To keep up with her busy release schedule check her website at www.jeannestjames.com or sign up for her newsletter: http://www.jeannestjames.com/newslettersignup

www.jeannestjames.com
jeanne@jeannestjames.com

Blog: http://jeannestjames.blogspot.com
Newsletter: http://www.jeannestjames.com/newslettersignup
Jeanne's Down & Dirty Book Crew: https://www.facebook.com/groups/JeannesReviewCrew/

facebook.com/JeanneStJamesAuthor
twitter.com/JeanneStJames
amazon.com/author/jeannestjames
instagram.com/JeanneStJames
bookbub.com/authors/jeanne-st-james
goodreads.com/JeanneStJames
pinterest.com/JeanneStJames

Get a FREE Erotic Romance Sampler Book

This book contains the first chapter of a variety of my books. This will give you a taste of the type of books I write and if you enjoy the first chapter, I hope you'll be interested in reading the rest of the book.

Each book I list in the sampler will include the description of the book, the genre, and the first chapter, along with links to find out more. I hope you find a book you will enjoy curling up with!

Get it here: BookHip.com/MTQQKK

www.ingramcontent.com/pod-product-compliance
Lightning Source LLC
Chambersburg PA
CBHW021321190726

48288CB00003B/905